EVERYBODY WANTS AN Oscar

The Hollywood Murder Mysteries

PETER S. FISCHER

THE GROVE POINT PRESS
Pacific Grove, California

Also by Peter S. Fischer

THE BLOOD OF TYRANTS

THE TERROR OF TYRANTS

The Hollywood Murder Mysteries

JEZEBEL IN BLUE SATIN

WE DON'T NEED NO STINKING BADGES

LOVE HAS NOTHING TO DO WITH IT

To Sandy Quinn
...for many years my own
personal Glenda Mae....

CHAPTER ONE

Fifty thousand dollars.

I think about that number. I roll it around on my tongue. I look into the bathroom mirror and I repeat it. Seriously. Then speculatively. Then with a huge grin on my face.

Fifty thousand dollars.

Then I think of something else Barry has told me.

The next Norman Mailer. That's how he described me. This is even more intriguing than the money. I try to be realistic. Agents are famous for flights of hyperbole while sucking up to clients. Still and all, I can't completely dismiss the notion.

Barry Loeb represents me. He works for the William Morris Agency and he is a pleasant little fellow, full of verve and optimism and a full two inches shorter than the agency' president, Abe Lastfogel. At William Morris, this is a job requirement and cruel competitors sometimes refer to the agency as munchkin land. I am pretty sure Barry is good at his job. I am not positive because this is the first thing he has ever had to do for me and we are waiting for good news that will match Barry's enthusiasm.

He has sent my novel, 'A Family of Strangers', to Doubleday. His contact is not only a fellow Terrapin from the University of Maryland, he is also a fraternity brother. They have been doing business together for nine years. Barry has told me that a sale to his pal Ivan is a lead pipe cinch. I am on my way to becoming America's newest top tier novelist. Even as I regard myself in the mirror, face half covered with shaving cream, I am thinking Pulitzer and dare I think it, Nobel?

"Joe, did you die in there or something?" comes a voice from the other side of the bathroom door. It emanates from my beloved Bunny Lesher who I have been living with for the past year. She is my soulmate, my enamorata, my muse, everything but my wife. But that's a whole other story.

"In a minute," I call back, taking the razor to my face once again.

"I'm putting your eggs on," she says.

My heart skips a beat. I have a fifty-fifty chance that they will be edible. In any case I will eat them, washing them down with orange juice and a cup of highly suspect coffee. After a year of valiant effort, Bunny now considers herself to be a cook and who am I to discourage her, especially if I feel like sharing her bed in the evening to come.

By the time I reach the kitchen, dressed spiffily in my new grey gabardine suit from Brooks Brothers, my eggs are on a plate. They are hard-over as opposed to easy-over with the yolk dry and crumbly. The toast doesn't look half bad and Bunny has made a mistake somewhere because the coffee tastes very good. She hugs me with a kiss and I respond in kind.. She looks great in a red silk blouse and a white scarf around her neck and a tight fitting white cotton skirt that lovingly displays her assets. In a matter of minutes I will be on my way to my desk at Warner Brothers Studios where I serve as the number two man in the Publicity Department and Bunny will be heading for the offices of The Hollywood Reporter where she is Billy Wilkerson's number one journalist.

"Do you think you'll hear from Barry today?" she asks.

"Maybe," I say.

"Will you call him?"

"Nope. Don't want to appear anxious."

"But you are anxious."

"Yep. But I don't want him to know it."

"I think he already knows it," she says.

"Yep," I say. Gary Cooper has nothing on me.

"But if he already knows it, what's the problem?"

"Image."

"What's that supposed to mean?"

"It means I have to display an attitude of comme ci, comme ca, as if the publication of my book is a matter of total indifference to me. That way when Doubleday tells me to go fly a kite, I can pretend I never cared in the first place."

She stares at me in wonderment.

"Men," she mutters and wanders off into the bedroom to recheck her makeup for the third time this morning.

The Warner Brothers Studio lot is located in Burbank about ten minutes from my driveway. It is a jungle of sound stages, office buildings, bungalows and back lot facades standing in for everything from a Mexican village to Broadway, NYC. Some people call it a factory for second rate movies. I, who am paid almost adequately to publicly disagree, call it home. The past twenty-four months have been the happiest of my life.

As I walk through the door to my office, my secretary, Glenda Mae, one time homecoming queen at Ole Miss, greets me with her usual smile and words of cheery welcome. She's already laid out the Times and the trade papers on my desk and within a minute has brought me a steaming hot cup of her very special chickory laced coffee. I am relaxed because today is going to be easy. I have no film in production which requires hour by hour babysitting. Within a few weeks they will start filming my next assignment, "The Glass Menagerie", and I can only hope that the cast is not it's own kind of menagerie, populated with feral performers exhibiting monstrous egos. So far they've signed up Jane Wyman, Arthur Kennedy and Kirk Douglas. Negotiations are ongoing for someone to play the part of Amanda Wingfield, a delusional older woman with no real grip on day to day life. Ethel Barrymore seems to have the inside track. Miriam Hopkins is also in the mix.

Wyman is hot off of her Oscar-winning role in "Johnny Belinda" and I understand that once you've been bitten by Oscar, you want more. I think she sees the part of Laura as a shot at number two. Kennedy and Douglas are old pals. They worked together on a terrific indie called "Champion" which vaulted Douglas into the top tier of leading men. Both were Oscar-nominated and both lost, unfairly perhaps. I hear good things about Kennedy. As for Douglas I was briefly assigned to "Young Man With a Horn" earlier in the year. I found him to be direct and very professional. If you knew your job, he'd support you no matter what. If you dogged it, you were in for trouble. We have gotten along well. I see no reason to expect anything but cooperation.

Another plus on this assignment is my chance to meet and maybe chat with a genuine American literary legend, Tennessee Williams. It's his play, originally staged on Broadway in 1944, that has been adapted by Williams himself for the screen. I've spotted him once or twice in the past week in the commissary, always with a crowd and always holding forth like the icon he is. I'm awaiting my opportunity to corner him alone.

I hear the phone ring and moments later, Glenda Mae buzzes

me on the intercom. Mr. Berger would like to see me in his office. I get up and start toward the other end of the corridor. Charlie Berger is my boss. He's been with the studio since the days of Bebe Daniels and Frank Fay and the arrival of newcomers like Eddie Robinson and Jimmy Cagney. His first job for the studio involved denying that "Little Caesar" was all about Al Capone while making sure that the audiences knew that it was. No one knows how old Charlie is but his skinny frame and white hair scream sixty and then some. It's rumored he'll be quitting at the end of the year. It's also rumored that I'm getting his job.

He grins at me from behind his desk but doesn't get up.

"How goes the battle, young Lochinvar?" he asks. Charlie talks like that once in a while. It's usually a reflection of the book he is currently reading. I tell him all is well. Bunny is well. And more than that, I'm enjoying a leisurely pace I haven't experienced in months.

"Well, don't get too complacent. I've decided to let you deal with Eleanor Parker."

I nod, unsure of where this is going. Eleanor Parker is the actress. Eleanor Powell is the tap dancer. Powell is married to Glenn Ford. Parker is married to a guy named Bert Friedlob. Still America has trouble telling them apart.

"What's the deal?" I ask.

"Parker's picture opened three weeks ago and she's been reading her reviews."

"Never a good sign," I observe.

"Some of the knuckle headed columnists are talking Oscar and Eleanor is taking it seriously. Well, maybe not Eleanor herself but her husband Bert is starting to beat the drum."

I nod again. "Caged" is a woman's prison picture, melodramatic and borderline cheesy but it's entertaining, doing good business, and Eleanor's personal notices are excellent. But Oscar? That seems like a big stretch. Besides Oscar contenders are released late in the year, not in May.

"How do you want me to handle it?" I ask.

"Put out the releases, lather her up with soft soap and hope that she forgets the whole thing before summer sets in."

"This I can handle. And if Bert gets pushy?"

"Smile a lot," Charlie says.

"Can do," I assure him.

At this moment the door to Charlie's office opens and the grand potentate of the studio swoops in unannounced.

Jack Warner is a dapper man with a pencil mustache, thinning hair and an aura that bespeaks raw power. He can be a paragon of charm and civility. He can also be a great white shark with sharp teeth with which to shred his enemies and to rectify the merest slight to his reputation. Today good fellowship seems to be oozing from every pore even as the noxious fumes from his Cuban cigar threaten to asphyxiate everyone in the room.

Charlie rises from his chair. "Good morning, Jack," he says.

I, too, rise to my feet. "Good morning, Mr. Warner," I gulp.

Warner fixes me with a mock scowl. "Listen, Bernardi, if you're going to be taking over this office later this year, you're going to have to stop quaking in your loafers every time I walk into a room. It's Jack or it's J.L. Are we clear about that?"

"Yes, sir," I say firmly as if responding to a drill sergeant. I add, "I mean, Jack."

He nods. "Good. Keep it that way." He turns to include Charlie. "Well, boys, I bring you good news. We have our Amanda Wingfield," he says proudly.

Charlie beams. "Great news, Jack. Who?"

"That son of a bitch Billy Wilder, yanking Swanson off the

trash heap and putting her in the so-called comeback part of the year. What's it called? Sunset Strip?"

"Boulevard," I say.

"Right. 'Sunset Boulevard.' And that other son of a bitch, Zanuck, replacing Colbert with Bette Davis who hasn't had a decent picture in five years, not since 'The Corn is Green.' I oughta know. I produced them. What a bunch of stinkers."

Now that I know who we are not getting I'm almost rabid to know who we have signed, Warner grins. It's not Barrymore or Hopkins because they are old news and this is somebody new. I'm terrified he's going to say 'Guess!' because I haven't a clue.

"Well, screw those boys. I've got my own old babe. Gertrude Lawrence."

As Charlie and I exchange a look, I think Warner is waiting for applause. Charlie jumps right in.

"Brilliant, Jack," he says. "A real coup."

I smile. "I never would have thought of it," I say, which is about as truthful as I can get without jeopardizing my job.

"She was up for the Davis part in 'All About Eve' but Zanuck nixed her. Big mistake. You want to talk about comebacks, we've got the big one. And I'll tell you something else, boys. This part with Lawrence in it has Oscar written all over it."

Yes, and maybe my future has heart attack written all over it. Miss Lawrence is a major theatrical talent although it's been said that in recent years her voice has occasionally deserted her and at times she has a propensity to sing flat. Since there are no songs in 'Menagerie', this will not be a problem. However, as a singer of not-quite-operatic range, she has a temperament to match the New York Met's most egotistical diva. Or so I have heard. I have also heard that directors quake at the thought of dealing with her eccentricities, wardrobe people walk on egg shells in her presence and cast and crew members give her a wide berth whenever she walks in the stage door. As I say, this is what I have heard, perhaps unfairly. Many who are perfectionists gain this reputation when they know their job and those around them don't. I can only wait and see. I doubt that director Irving Rapper will put up with much nonsense. I know for a fact that Kirk Douglas won't.

We chat for a few more minutes. Naturally Warner wants a full court press on this. Releases, photos, special events, interviews, awards. Leave nothing out. If flattery and persuasion don't work, try bribery. He's only half kidding. By the time we're through the name of Gertrude Lawrence should be on the tip of the tongue of every movie goer in America.

A few minutes later I am walking slowly back to my office. Although I am not a casting maven, I do have some sense of reality. Amanda Wingfield is an overweight, blue collar hausfrau living in St. Louis, Missouri, with her son and crippled daughter. She sells magazine subscriptions to help keep the family afloat. She is dowdy and delusional, a working class woman unable to cope with life's realities. To play this part, Jack Warner has signed a darling of the British and American musical stage, a confidant of Noel Coward, a sophisticated world traveler and a grand dame of the world's literati. While Amanda might be cooking mulligan stew on her wood burning stove in her delapidated kitchen, Gertrude would walk out of any restaurant that dared serve it.

I see trouble ahead. Wyman probably considers the role of Laura as her passport to a second Oscar. Jack Warner sees an Oscar for Lawrence in the other showy part even though she seems all wrong for it. And to make things worse, Eleanor Parker wants us to hype her for her nitty-gritty prison picture. I can only hope that June Haver doesn't show up looking for an Oscar nod for 'The Daughter of Rosie O'Grady'.

As I walk into the anteroom to my office, Glenda Mae rolls her eyes and nods toward my door. "The little guy is here," she whispers. I think maybe she has a fear of midgets.

Barry Loeb, my agent, is sitting in my guest chair, a rolled up screenplay in his hand. He gets up as I enter but I shoo him back down.

"How are you this morning, Barry?" I ask.

"Been better," he says glumly. I look at him incredulously. For Barry this is the equivalent of saying, 'Just found out I have cancer.'

"What?" I say, frowning.

"You ever hear of a screenplay called 'No Home of My Own'?" he asks.

I shake my head no.

"RKO optioned this novel about two months ago. Written by someone named V.J. Shelley."

"Never heard of him," I say.

"Me, either," Barry responds."They put one of their staffers on it and he whips up a screenplay which has been floating around the agencies for the past couple of weeks, sniffing for maybe a new face to play the lead. They can't put Bob Mitchum in all their pictures. Anyway my buddy Sid Weiss had a copy on his desk so I picked it up out of curiosity and started to skim through it. Would you like to hear the plot?"

"Not particularly."

"Oh, I think you'll want to hear this," he says. "Young kid living in a foster home, miserable, picked on, abused. Runs away to work in the oil fields of Texas, meets the beautiful daughter of the owner, they fall in love. She gets pregnant. Old man's furious, sends a couple of his guys to rough him up but in the fight, one of the goons gets killed and the young man has to run for it---"

"Wait a minute," I cut in, confused and a little anxious. "That's my novel."

Barry nods. "Right, Joe," he says, "that's your novel."

CHAPTER TWO

I look at Barry, my eyes hooded like a cobra. My novel, which has cost me six years of my life, has been unashamedly stolen by some person named V.J. Shelley whom I do not know and who I do not wish to know except maybe to punch his lights out. Which, by the way, I am perfectly capable of doing providing he is no taller than my agent.

Barry is perceptive. He senses that I am angry.

"Besides me, who else has read it?" he asks. I continue to stare at him, a thousand thoughts of mayhem rattlling around in my brain. "Joe, look at me," he says. "Concentrate. Who else has read the manuscript?"

Finally it sinks in what he is asking.

"Bunny," I say.

"Did she take it with her to her office?"

"No, she read it at the house."

"Okay. Who else?" he asks.

"Ed North."

Barry screws up his face. "Ed North? The Ed North? Edmund North, the writer?"

"Yes."

"How'd that happen?"

"He was here on the lot when they were filming 'Flamingo Road'. He'd adapted Robert Wilder's novel for the screen and we got to chatting one day and I told him about my book. He said he'd love to read it. Well, you don't pass up an offer like that and so I sent him a copy. Right away I heard back from him. He liked it a great deal and wondered if I'd mind if he sent it to Wilder, Wilder being a novelist while Ed was a screenwriter. I said sure. I'd be honored."

"Wilder also read it," Barry says.

"I don't know," I say. "After a couple of months when Ed didn't hear back, he gave Wilder a call. Wilder denied ever receiving it. We assume it got lost in the mail."

"That's one explanation," Barry observes cynically.

I shake my head. "A fine author like Robert Wilder isn't going to steal my book. Besides the name on the screenplay is V.J. Shelley."

"And Sam Clemens never heard of Mark Twain," Barry says.

"Won't fly, Barry. Something else is going on."

I leaf absentmindedly through the screenplay that Barry has handed me. "You know," I say, "maybe we ought to pay a visit to RKO and get to the bottom of this. Who's in charge over there?"

He shrugs. "As of yesterday Sam Bischoff but this morning, maybe Jane Russell. Who knows? Ever since Howard Hughes bought the place two years ago, you can't tell who's who without a scorecard."

I nod. I'd heard that about RKO. All the stability of the Italian parliament. "Let's go see Sam while he still has a job."

I start for the door as Barry slowly gets to his feet, all apologies. "Gee, Joe, I'd like to but Abe's got this ten o'clock in the conference room. All hands on deck. Definitely a do not miss."

I look him in the eye and he looks sheepishly over at the autographed picture of Livvy DeHaviland on my wall. I know he is lying because when it comes to backbone, Barry's a little short on vertebrae. I hear he's a good negotiator but no agent wants to be in a room where a studio chief may be harangued by an irate author with God, and possibly the law, on his side. I clap Barry on the shoulder, tell him to give Abe my best and promise to let him know what transpires. I'm sure Barry thinks I'm a little nuts but I look at it this way. Howard Hughes doesn't sign my paycheck, Jack Warner does. And there's nothing Jack Warner likes better than a good fight, especially if it gives him a chance to piss all over another studio.

I'm headed for Gower Street where RKO houses its sound stages and offices. It is now, as it has always been, a studio in search of an identity. The big ape, King Kong, put them on the map. When follow-up ape features didn't fare as well, they leaned on Astaire and Rogers to keep the doors open. At the same time Cary Grant and Kate Hepburn were turning screwball comedies into an art form. In 1941 Orson Welles nearly put them out of business with 'Citizen Kane' and when the war broke out, the studio's contribution to the war effort was a potpourri of films about The Falcon and Tarzan. After the war, production chief Dore Schary assuaged his Jewish guilt by producing grim message pictures like 'Crossfire'. Enter Hughes in 1948, exit Schary for the top job at MGM. Jane Russell started working regularly and what is next for this studio is anyone's guess.

Without an appointment I'm at the mercy of the receptionist and ultimately, Sam Bischoff's secretary who tells me that Sam is in a meeting in Howard Hughes' bedroom. I find this odd but keep my mouth shut. It will be at least another two hours or it could be all day. There's no way of knowing. She asks if someone else might be able to help me. I say sure. Whoever's in charge of acquiring intellectual properties. She looks at me funny so I say novels and screenplays. She smiles and punches a button in her intercom system and a few minutes later I find myself in the office of Chaz Lambo.

Although Bischoff makes the final determination, Lambo is the guy who makes the recommendations based on input from his staff who often get their insight from their secretaries or interns or perhaps even from the wives and lovers of said secretaries and interns. Hollywood is a lot like Congress. Lawmakers pass laws without reading them, studios do the same thing, relying most often on something called "coverage". This is normally a one or two page synopsis of the plot of the book or script, obviously omitting nuance of character and beauty of language. In the days of the silents producers like Sennett and Roach would film movies based on this sort of scanty input. I'm pleased to see how far we have come in the past twenty-three years.

Lambo is young, maybe even younger than me but he's built like Humpty Dumpty and the hair on his head is thin to the point of non-existent. He smiles a lot in a friendly manner and when he laughs, it's more like a giggle but you can't help liking the guy.

"My guys in publicity say your guys over at Warners do a helluva job," he says. I thank him without pointing out that two of my guys are gals. I'm not here to pick nits. "So what can I do for you, Joe?" he asks."Looking for a job?" he giggles.

I shake my head. "A couple of months ago you optioned a novel called 'No Home of My Own'."

"Did we?" It seems to ring no bells.

"You put a couple of screenwriters on it and two weeks ago you started sending copies out to the agencies."

"Possible," he nods. "That's how we work when we find something we like."

"Then you remember it?"

"Not really," he confesses. "We have a lot of stuff in the pipeline. What's your interest, Joe?"

"Your screenplay is based on my novel," I say.

"Really? You are V.J. Shelley?" Lambo asks.

Aha, I think to myself. Of course he remembers, the slimy shark. I withdraw my previous endorsement.

"No, I am Joseph F.X. Bernardi and V.J. Shelley is a no-good plagarizing son of a bitch."

"Whoa, there, Joe. That's quite an accusation."

"I understand that and I also understand that you may know absolutely nothing about it. Nonetheless it's true."

"And you have proof?"

"I have a carbon copy."

Lambo shrugs. "Anybody can type."

"What's that supposed to mean?"

"Only that any schlub with a Royal Standard can re-type the contents of a book and then claim someone has stolen his material. Joe, we see it all the time. Con artists looking to make a quick buck. Not you, of course, but others with no scruples. I believe you."

"Thanks," I say.

"Our legal department, however, may have a different view. As I recall we laid out $5,000 in option money with another $20,000 due if the picture gets made and of course, a healthy percentage of the net profits."

Which, in Hollywood bookkeeping, is a healthy percentage of nothing. But he knows that and he knows that I know that so we don't waste time haggling the point.

"So if I am right, which I am, RKO is liable to be out five thousand bucks which they may or may not be able to get back through the courts," I say.

"Exactly," he says, "so I ask you again, Joe, have you any proof that this book is actually your work?"

"Well, my girlfriend's read it----" He nods, smiling. "And my agent has read it----" He nods again and the smile gets broader. "And it's also been read by Edmund North." The smile suddenly evaporates.

"Edmund North, the screenwriter?" he asks warily.

"Yes, several months ago," I reply.

Again he starts to nod. No smile this time.

"What was he like?" I ask.

"Who?"

"Shelley."

"Never met him," Lambo says. "Everything came through his agent."

"Who's that?"

"Maybelle Ruskin."

"Never heard of her," I say.

"Neither had I until we made this deal. She runs a one-woman agency out of a tiny office in a building in West Hollywood."

"Okay," I say, "then what is SHE like?"

"No idea. I never met her. It was all done by mail and phone."

"But you know where her office is."

Lambo shrugs. "We checked her out from top to bottom. When we realized she was about one step up from Poverty Alley, we threw a lowball offer at her and she took it. No haggling. No arguing. Anybody else the numbers would have been double."

I nod and rise from my chair. "Well, Chaz, I suggest you put your legal people on notice and if you like, check out Ed

North for confirmation. Meantime, I am going to pay a visit to this Maybelle Ruskin and I promise you one thing. One way or another I am going to reclaim my novel and my good name, whatever it takes, even if I have to choke the son of a bitch til he's blue in the face."

Lambo nods. "Sure, Joe. I get it. You're pissed. Guess I would be, too." He turns to a filing cabinet behind his desk. He opens a drawer and takes out a file folder.

"You're going to need an address," he says.

Traffic is light and soon I am looking up at a rundown three-story office building on Highland near the intersection with Beverly Boulevard. It looks like something out of the 1920's that was abandoned at birth by its mother. Most of the windows are filthy and those that have gilt lettering have an aura of desperation. I park at curbside and go into the lobby. I search for a directory. There is none. I check the mailboxes. M. Ruskin is located on the third floor. The elevator, predictably, sports a sign which reads 'Out of Order'. The sign is affixed permanently to the elevator door handle by rust. I find the staircase and climb.

The sign on 305 reads "Maybelle Ruskin, Literary Agent and Career Consultant". I try the doorknob. It turns. I enter. The first thing that strikes me is the smell of mold. I am in a small ante-room. A section of one wall is devoted to photos, awards and citations but aside from that, every square inch of wall space is lined with book shelves, every shelf stacked with books most of them old. This lady is in the wrong business. She should start a lending library.

There is a small sofa to the left. Alongside is a table with a lamp and a large glass jar of jellybeans. In the center of the room is a small round table on which sits a collection of five slim volumes held in place by bookends. I check them out. They are all written by V.J. Shelley. On the far side of the room is a door, slightly ajar. I think I can hear someone singing 'Un Bel Di Vedremo" from 'Madame Butterfly'. I cross the room and peer in.

Maybelle Ruskin is an imposing woman standing beside an unwashed window, book in hand and reading in the lousy light. She is wearing a voluminous orange kaftan that approximates the color of her hair. Off in the corner I see the record player. The volume is low but I can clearly hear Madame B. wondering when Lieutenant P. is coming back to sweep her off her feet.

I clear my throat discreetly, always a better approach than "Hey, You!". She doesn't respond so I do it again, more loudly. She turns toward me and raises a curious eyebrow.

"I hate to interrupt," I say.

"But you have, young man. Never mind, come in anyway." She flips her book shut and glides toward me as if floating on ball bearings, hand extended. "Maybelle Ruskin," she says as we shake.

"Joe Bernardi," I say.

"And what do you write, Joseph? Ballades, couplets, iambic, blank verse, pindaric. No, no, let me guess. I say you are an epigramarian."

I shake my head. "Sorry. Novelist."

Her face falls five stories. "Oh," she says. "I'm so sorry. I don't do novels."

"Not even 'No Home of My Own'?" I say.

Her face lights up. "Ah, you have me there," she says and then looks puzzled. "But how do you know the book? It's not scheduled for publication until the holidays."

"I've read the screenplay," I tell her.

"Not the same thing at all," she says testily. "Like comparing filet mignon to flank steak."

"Tell me about Mr. Shelley," I say.

"Ginny?" she asks.

"Ginny?" I say, caught off guard.

"Virginia Jenks. The Shelley was added to her nom de plume as an homage to her favorite poet."

"Homage," I mutter without enthusiasm.

"Ginny is a marvelous talent and a gentle soul, the dear child. Frankly I was so caught up in her poetic prowess, it never occurred to me that she would have such a powerful novel locked in her bosom."

"She didn't," I say.

Maybelle looks at me askance.

"It took me six long years but I am responsible for every word, every comma and every period. In a word, Miss Ruskin, your gentle soul is a thief."

"Impossible," she utters.

"Afraid not," I say.

Maybelle turns slowly and returns to the window, looking out on Highland Avenue. "I cannot believe it," she says quietly. "I will not believe it. And yet---" She turns to look at me. "There is so much that Ginny is, but there is also much that she is not. For one thing, she is not a typist. Hasn't a clue. Everything she submits is in longhand." Maybelle sighs. "Oh, dear, the poor child. I know how desperately she wanted to be thought of as something more than a little known poetess, but this? I don't know what to say. I wanted to believe she'd written 'No Home of My Own', but honest writing often involves chronicling one's life experience. The life described in 'No Home of My Own' is not hers."

"No," I say. "It's mine."

Maybelle nods. "Yes, I can see it in your face and in your eyes."

"I'd like to talk to her."

"Of course." She hesitates. "When I say she is a gentle soul, Mr. Bernardi, I mean just that. She's young, she's very frail and she suffers terribly from stomach ulcers which flare up when she is stressed. Twice she needed to be hospitalized. No, I'm sorry, Mr. Bernardi, it won't do for you to browbeat her."

"That is not my intention, Miss Ruskin. I just want to get my book back. I will speak softly and soothingly, I promise."

Maybelle nods and goes to her desk, opens the drawer and takes out a couple of tickets which she hands to me. "She's reading selections from her poems at The Jabberwocky tonight at eight o'clock. It's a coffee house on Western Avenue. It's not a big place and it crowds up quickly. Get there early if you can."

I thank her for the tickets and assure her that I will behave civilly. On my way through the anteroom I glance at the wall near the door and my eye is caught by a framed promotional flyer hanging among the vanity photos. The flyer advertised poetry readings by Virginia Jenks on radio station KFI-FM every night at midnight between last Christmas and New Years. In the center of the flyer is her photo. She has a thin face, too thin, and her features are plain. She wears her ash blonde hair straight and long down to her shoulders. I would never give her a second look except that there is something about her eyes. They are haunting and they give her visage a sweet and innocent aura. I am drawn to her and I ask myself, is this the face of a thief? And if not, what kind of a face is it?

CHAPTER THREE

'm back at the studio by twelve-thirty. I hustle up the staircase to the second floor, hoping to phone Bunny at her desk before she ducks out for lunch. As I approach my office, Eleanor Parker and her husband Bert are just coming out. When she sees me she smiles broadly and hurries to me, favoring me with non-existent air kisses on each cheek.

"Joe! We were hoping to catch you in. Have you got a minute?" she asks.

Sure, I say, greeting Bert with a handshake. We go into my office. I offer refreshments but they're not interested. I ask Glenda Mae to pour me a cup of coffee. When we are comfortably settled around my desk, I congratulate Eleanor on her marvelous performance in 'Caged'. She accepts the compliment graciously and tells me that 'Caged' is the reason for her visit.

"So many kind people have complimented me, it's been a wonderful experience."

Bert jumps in. "I think what Eleanor is trying to say is that this outpouring of love has touched her deeply and she is starting to think of this film and her role as something more than just a movie. It's an opportunity to convert these good wishes into something more substantial in the way of honoring the studio."

"We're talking Oscar here," I suggest.

"Exactly!" Bert says, pounding his fist for emphasis.

Eleanor smiles demurely. "Nothing would make me happier than to deliver an Academy Award to Jack Warner as my thanks for all the confidence he has shown in me."

Glenda Mae brings in my hot mug of coffee and my two lumps of sugar and places them neatly on my desk.

"As for me personally," Eleanor says, "the Oscar isn't all that important. As an artist the reward is in the work."

As Glenda Mae goes out, shutting the door, she raises her eyes to heaven. I catch her look as she shakes her head.

"Eleanor's absolutely right," Bert says. "It's all about the work. Eleanor doesn't need any statuette to tell her she's done a good job."

"Of course not," I say.

"On the other hand," Bert says, "there's something tangible about an Oscar, something you can point to with pride for years to come."

"I understand one of the previous winners is using hers as a doorstop," I say.

"Well, now, that's criminal," Eleanor says. "Just criminal."

"Here's what we were thinking," Bert says. "An all out publicity blitz, starting slowly but intensifying right after Labor Day with full page ads in the trades, radio interviews. photo spreads in some of the fan magazines and so on and so forth."

"Sounds like a plan," I say.

"The only question we have," Bert says, "is whether we should leave everything to the studio or hire an outside publicist. This is where we need your input."

I smile in understanding. "Your choice, of course, Bert, but I can assure you I am prepared to do everything possible to beef up Eleanor's chances of a nomination and a win."

Eleanor smiles at me. She is glowing. "Thank you, Joe. That's exactly what I told Bert but I think he needed to hear it from you personally." She looks at her husband. "Darling?"

Bert throws up his hands. "That's good enough for me." He gets up and reaches across the desk to shake my hand. "Looking forward to working with you, Joe. I've got a lot of really good ideas."

Eleanor favors me with a couple more air kisses and off they go, content that they are in good hands. I am pleased by the faith they have in me. They are pleased that they won't be spending many thousands of dollars on an outside firm. Everybody wins except maybe me when Bert starts to drag out some of those really good ideas of his.

I grab the phone and dial Bunny. I'm lucky. She's getting ready to go out the door with her lunch pals, Ginger and Marvin. I tell her I'm taking her out tonight for supper and a show.

"Oh, goodie," she squeals. "A date. What show?"

"It's a surprise," I say. "How about if I pick you up at the magazine around six?"

"But I have to get dressed," she complains.

"You are dressed," I say.

She is getting suspicious. "Hey, what kind of date is this?"

"It's a date with the tall handsome fella who loves you more than anything else in the world."

"Really? I thought the date was with you."

Ha ha. By now I should know better than to feed her straight lines.

"Six o'clock. Main entrance. Be there," I say in my most domineering voice. I hang up. I guess I have made myself clear. I also know that it will be at least 6:15 before she appears. Bunny always has the last word.

I realize I'm hungry so I head off to the commissary to grab a bite. I'll probably buy a sandwich and bring it back to my desk. I hate eating alone in the commissary. I'm invariably accosted by all sorts of people who want something from me. But when I walk in the door, I spot Tennessee Williams and another man sitting quietly at a table near the back of the room drinking coffee. No time like the present to do a little accosting of my own. I may never get a better chance.

As I approach, Williams looks up curiously. I toss him my friendliest smile. "Mr. Williams?" I put out my hand. "Joe Bernardi, studio publicity."

He returns my smile and takes my hand.

"How do you do, Mr. Bernardi." He gestures to the man with him. "My good friend Frank Merlo." We shake. Merlo's young, dark, good looking with a pleasant smile.

"I've been assigned to publicize 'The Glass Menagerie'," I tell him.

"Delighted," Williams says. "Would you care to join us?"

"Thanks, I would," I say as I sit.

"We have already ordered lunch but I'm sure there would be no problem getting you something." He waves an immaculately manicured hand in the direction of Clarisse, my favorite waitress, who hurries toward us. I order my club sandwich and coffee and settle back.

"So tell me, Joe, how long have you been beating the drums for this wonderful studio?" Williams asks.

"Just over two years, Mr. Williams----"

He cuts me off with a wave of his hand. "No, no, none of that. If we are to work together, then it must be Tom."

I nod with a smile. "Tom."

"And what do you think of our little project so far, Joe?" he asks, draining the remains of his coffee. Merlo looks over at the empty cup and takes it as he gets up.

"I'll get you a refill," Merlo says. He hurries off.

Williams smiles. "Dear boy." He looks at me, sizing me up, looking for a reaction and maybe some sign of bigotry. "A lovely young man, an excellent companion. I don't know what I'd do without him."

I nod. "I would say you are a very lucky man, Tom."

"Well said, sir. Indeed I am." Williams speaks softly with a languid Southern drawl. "As I was saying, our project. Your opinion, Joe?"

I shrug. "We have an excellent script, a topnotch cast and a wonderful director in Irving Rapper."

Williams smiles. "One out of three. I suppose it could be worse."

"Meaning?"

"Meaning that Mr. Rapper is a most gifted director."

"But what about the script? You wrote it."

"I did," he says, "with the dubious assistance of a co-writer whose name happily escapes me at this moment. On orders from someone high up he has added a sugary ending which has nothing to do with my play. If I wanted to write happy endings I would have applied for a job at MGM writing for Andy Hardy."

Merlo returns with the coffee and resumes his seat. He has said practically nothing, preferring to exist anonymously in Williams' shadow.

"And the cast. We've got some darned good people, Tom," I point out.

"An excellent array of talent. Miss Wyman, a joy to be with. Mr. Douglas and Mr. Kennedy, bright and excellent conversationalists."

"And Gertrude Lawrence?"

Williams leans back in is chair and tents his fingers thoughtfully before responding.

"Miss Lawrence is a highly talented musical hall diva, a masterful comedienne with an adequate non-operatic singing voice. How anyone could mistake her for poor pathetic Amanda Wingfield is beyond me but that is why I am a writer, Joe, and not a producer. The Amanda of my imagination is perfect in every way."

"Then you think she can't handle it?"

"She is a dandelion in a basket of daisies, a tugboat in a flotilla of yachts, Helen Keller in a choir of choristers. I fear that my co-writer whose name continues to escape me will tinker with the role so as to bring Amanda closer to Gertrude and not the other way around. If, as I fear, the script suddenly develops a scene where Amanda breaks into a chorus of 'I've Got a Lovely Bunch of Coconuts', I will remove my name from the credits, train back to Mississippi and spent the summer drinking myself into oblivion."

"I see," I say.

"See, but do not remember," Williams says. "This is all off the record, the ravings of a betrayed artist. When hyping this film as the so-called first major hit of the new decade, don't let my negativity color your judgement. Now, on to more pleasant subjects," he continues. "Are you married, Joe, and if so, why?"

We spend the next half hour talking of personal things. He and Frank will be leaving in a few days to spend the summer in Key West while I will be spending the dog days at my desk pounding out a never ending stream of repetitious "news flashes" about our stars. I envy Williams his mobility and think that if we can get this plagarism thing worked out and the book is a success, Bunny and I can enjoy the same kind of freedom.

Tis a blessing devoutly to be sought.

CHAPTER FOUR

At precisely 6:17 Bunny emerges from the front entrance of the offices of The Hollywood Reporter, waving cheerily and without guile. By my watch she is two minutes late for our 6:00 rendezvous. She gets in, slides across the seat and kisses me like she means it. Hell, Bunny always means it. I power away from the curb in my six cylinder Ford coupe determined to recoup some of my manhood.

"I am so excited," she says, rubbing her hands together.

"Well, don't expect too much. This is a kind of avant garde thing," I say.

She stops smiling and gives me the fisheye. "What's that supposed to mean?" she says.

"I mean, we're not going to see 'Where's Charley?' at the Greek."

She shrugs. "Without Ray Bolger, who cares? What else are we not going to see?"

"Shut up, woman, and let me surprise you," I growl. "And by the way, we are not dining at Chasen's."

"It's okay, I hate Chasen's," she says. She falls silent for a moment and then she asks, "What do you hear from Barry?"

I look at her sharply. "Why do you ask?"

"I don't know," she says. "Maybe because we're going on this date so you can let me down easy when you tell me Doubleday passed on your book."

"They didn't," I say.

"Good," she says.

"It's worse," I say.

When she fixes me with a troubled stare I tell her the whole ugly story from start to finish. Her face turns grimmer and grimmer.

"So we're going to this poetry reading tonight so that, what? You can throttle this thieving bitch with your bare hands?"

"Unlikely it will go that far," I say.

"If you can't handle it, macho man, I can," she says.

"Why don't we start off polite and conciliatory and see where that leads us," I say.

"Good idea," Bunny says, "and after we do that, I'll punch her lights out."

I glance over at her. She means it.

Biff's All American Diner is a converted railroad dining car situated on Crenshaw Boulevard just south of Wilshire Boulevard and a stone's throw from the Wilshire Country Club. The flashing red neon sign, "EATS", is designed to lure hungry travelers inside the doors. Ditto for the somewhat smaller sign, "MOM'S HOME COOKING". I happen to know that Biff's Mom is doing five-to-ten at the California Institution for Women at Tehachapi for passing about fifteen thousand bucks worth of bad paper and the only things she ever learned to cook were the books.

If Bunny is disappointed by the blue-collar surroundings she gives no sign and when she looks at the menu, she becomes downright animated.

"Mmmm, meat loaf," she purrs. "And fried chicken, mashed potatoes and corn." She looks around and sniffs the air. "Something smells good too."

"Pot roast," I say. "Biff's specialty, and guaranteed to be good as long as Ling Wu is still working here." Ling is Biff's long time cook. Ling is "Mom". Our waitress comes to the table and after we establish that Ling is, indeed, still in the kitchen, we both order the pot roast with mashed potatoes, string beans and brown gravy.

While we are waiting for our food, I feed nickels into the wall mounted remote access juke box that's hooked up to the giant Seeburg against the far wall. This is a brand new innovation and Biff is one of the first to have it. I punch in B12, D15, and E11 which will bring up 'Mona Lisa' with Nat King Cole, 'It Isn't Fair', sung by Don Cornell and the Ames Brothers doing 'Sentimental Me'. Bunny's a sucker for weepies and I'm softening her up for later this evening.

"Well, I have news," Bunny says with a grin. "I'm leaving you."

This is news. I glower at her. "Really? When?"

"Tomorrow," she says.

"Hey, what's your hurry?" I say. "Soon as we eat we'll go home and get you packed and have you on the road by midnight."

She sticks her tongue out at me. "I have a reservation on TWA for a ten o'clock flight to New York."

"Well, at least you're running away in style," I say. "And when did you make this momentous decision?"

"I didn't. Billy did. And it was early this afternoon." Billy Wilkerson is the editor and publisher of The Hollywood Reporter and Bunny's boss.

"There's a publisher's convention at the Waldorf. Billy was supposed to go but he got hung up with some crisis and I got elected. By the way, wanna come?"

"Wow!" I say. "I'd love to but I have a slight case of plagiarism I have to deal with."

"Your loss," she says.

"Don't I know," I say.

We get off my troubles and onto her upcoming trip. She's excited. New York is always fun but more than that, she's starting to feel a lot of self-worth. Billy has faith in her. That counts for a lot. I don't say it in so many words but I am proud of her and she knows how I feel.

We get to The Jabberwocky around quarter of and Maybelle has it right. It's a small place, already crowding up. There are a few tables and chairs but there are also huge pillows strewn around facing a tiny platform with a lectern on it, lit by a spot. I buy two large mugs of cappuccino at the counter and we snuggle into a large pillow in the corner closest to the stage. The placard by the door had read "Virginia Jenks, Poetess, 8:00". Her photo is slightly different. She seems thinner but with that same haunted look in her eyes. At one minute to eight, the proprietor, a mousy little brown-skinned man, takes to the tiny stage and introduces her and she enters from the side. She is barely five-two if that and wears a simple sack like dress offset by several chains of beads hanging around her neck. She carries a small volume in her right hand.

She starts to read. I scan the crowd. They are enthralled and respectfully quiet in a mellow sort of way. Their dress is unusual. I see a lot of caftans and muu-muus, fringed leather shirts and jackets, beads of every shape and size, turquoise everywhere. The men mostly wear their hair very long and I sense, very unwashed. I spot an older woman sitting near the rear who looks terribly out of place. Her greying hair is neatly permed, her makeup meticulously applied, and she is wearing a conservative pale yellow silk suit. Atop her head is an odd looking yellow straw hat adorned with pink tea roses interspersed with tiny bluebirds.. She, too, is totally focused on the words of Virginia Jenks. I guess poetry lovers come in all shapes and sizes.

She is not smoking but half the room is and what I am smelling is not Virginia tobacco. I hope that when we leave I will be able to drive. I look over at Bunny. She is transfixed. Whatever this young woman is spouting is sparking something in Bunny's soul. As for me, poetry and I are strangers. I can get a belly laugh out of Lear or Nash and I adore limericks if they are dirty enough, but Millay and Dickinson leave me cold. Call me a cretin. It's the way I am.

Virginia is halfway through her second poem when I hear a commotion coming from out front. I hear a woman's voice shout, "Get out of my way, you little shit!" and as I turn, an attractive but determined woman in levis and a black leather jacket has just shoved the proprietor aside and is advancing through the crowd toward Virginia.

"Killer! Murdering bitch!" she shouts. "You killed my husband!" A quick witted man up front grabs at her leg as she goes by but she only kicks herself free and starts to mount the platform. I am close enough to see that she means business so I leap to my feet and cut her off just as she is closing her hands around Virginia's pencil thin neck. She struggles, trying to reach back to claw at my face but as quick as she is, there's Bunny grabbing her wrists and helping me drag her to the floor. Someone shouts, "Call the police!" while another goes in search of a stout rope with which to bind her until the cops come. Bunny goes to

Virginia's side. She has slumped to the floor and her expression is one of bewilderment. Willing hands are pitching in as the rope arrives and I join Bunny in getting Virginia to her feet and off-stage to a small office in back. After introducing ourselves, we sit her behind the desk as the proprietor hurries in, all aflutter. I tell him to bring water and he u-turns right back out again. Virginia is conscious but shaken as Bunny rubs her wrists and talks quietly to her.

The cops arrive ten minutes later and after hearing what happened from a chattering band of eyewitnesses, they take the woman into custody. As I watch them leave I notice the older woman in the yellow straw hat getting to her feet and following them out.

Meanwhile Virginia is faring much better and expresses her gratitude for our help. She's downed a glass of water and is now working on a cup of hot Turkish coffee. If that doesn't jolt her back to full comprehension, nothing will. Several members of the audience peer in to see if she's all right and satisfied, they leave. Soon there is no one left but the three of us and the proprietor whose name we learn is Bahadur Singh. He is ready to close up for the night but I convince him to stay open for another thirty minutes to give me a chance to talk to Virginia. I know she's had an ordeal but I have a lot of questions and they won't wait. He hesitates at first but when I hand him my card and promise him two tickets to the world premiere of 'Bright Leaf' with Gary Cooper, opening in a couple of weeks at the Pantages, he readily agrees and goes out front.

Virginia assures us she is all right and will be glad to answer any of our questions. Although Bunny has reservations, I don't and I plunge right in.

"Who was that woman?" I ask her, "and what was that all about?"

"Her name is Emma Schroeder. She's the wife---the estranged wife of the man I was in love with. Leon Schroeder, the man I lived with and the man I was going to marry."

"And I presume now that he is dead," I say.

"Yes. He died five months ago. Heart failure. I was at his side when he passed on."

"That woman seems to think it was something more than heart failure."

Virginia shakes her head violently. "She is wrong and her accusation is monstrous."

"Then why does she think----?"

"Because she is a pathetic jealous woman who was incapable of holding Leon's love. She may have beauty on the outside but her core is a barren mass of pulpish miasma."

Barren mass of pulpish miasma? What the hell does that mean, I think to myself.

"Well put, Virginia," Bunny says, holding her hand. I look at her sharply. Is there some language being spoken here with which I am not familiar?

"You're telling me she was not a very nice person," I say to Virginia.

She cocks her head at me and half smiles. "Yes, Mr. Bernardi, that is what I am saying." Dummy is what she is thinking.

"And of course, you did not kill him," I venture.

"I did not. I am a highly moral person, brought up by my parents to know the difference between right and wrong. The sixth Commandment instructs us, do not kill. The Commandments guide my life."

"Really," I say. "And how do you feel about number eight?"

"I also do not steal."

"How nice," I say. "Then tell me about your novel, Miss

Jenks, "No Home of My Own", soon to be a major motion picture." I can't help but let a little bitterness creep into my voice.

"How do you know about my novel?" she asks.

"I know about it because it isn't your novel, young lady. It's mine."

She looks at me in shock.

"Yours?"

"Mine."

"That's ridiculous," she says.

"I've been working on it for over six years. Bunny read a couple of dozen chapters almost a year ago and it wasn't your name on the title page."

Virginia struggles to her feet. "I am not going to listen to this."

She tries to push past me. I grab her arm.

"Joe! No." Bunny says in warning.

She's right. I can't bully this woman. I let her go. She gets to the door and turns back. "You are wrong, sir. The work is mine own, summoned up from the misty shadows of images long interred in the dusty sands of pubescent memory." And then she goes.

I think I know what she just said but I'm not sure. I look at Bunny who explains.

"She has written this relying on memories of her early unhappy life."

I shake my head. "The book is about a guy who sweats and toils in the oil fields of Texas, for God's sakes," I say.

"Maybe she's remembering another life she had before the one she's in now?" she suggests.

I give her a look. Now I have two dingbats on my hands.

CHAPTER FIVE

I drive Bunny back to her office so she can pick up her car and head home. I have a different agenda. If I can't get anything out of Ginny Jenks, maybe I'll have better luck with Emma Schroeder. Very possibly she is more pissed off at Jenks than I am. She may also know something about Jenks that I will be able to use to pry the truth from her about my book.

I'm pretty sure the two uniforms that dragged Emma Schroeder away were assigned to Metro Division. It's a big place but there's plenty of parking for visitors. As I start toward the main entrance the woman in the straw hat emerges looking none too happy. Now my curiosity is piqued and I consider jogging over to intercept her but even as I consider it, I'm too late. She gets into a late model DeSoto and drives off. I make a mental note to find out who that woman is.

Inside I check at the desk and at first the sergeant on duty doesn't know what I'm talking about. When I keep after him he makes a call and then tells me that the lady is in the second floor lockup. He points to the staircase and tells me to see Detective Moreno. I ask the sergeant about the woman in the straw hat but he's not much help. She'd wanted to go upstairs but was told to wait. After a few minutes, she apparently got tired of sitting around and left. No, the sergeant has no idea who she was.

I find Moreno at his desk typing up a report. He's a middle aged guy on the portly side with a healthy head of black hair and a bushy mustache. Like most cops he types with a couple of fingers and it's slow going. As I approach his desk I look past him to the far side of the squad room where Emma Schroeder is sitting quietly in the lockup.

"Detective Moreno?" I say. He looks up. "Joe Bernardi. I was at the coffee house when the incident occurred."

He sighs. "If you're here to give a statement, I don't need it. Got more than I can handle," he says.

"What's the charge?"

"Don't know," he says. "I'm waiting to see if the victim shows up to press charges. If she doesn't, we'll probably kick her loose."

"You mind if I talk to her?"

He regards me suspiciously. "About what?"

"Motive. I'd like to find out why she attacked the victim," I say.

"You a reporter?"

I shake my head. "Interested party. It's a long story."

"Got no time for long stories," Moreno says. He jams a thumb in the direction of the cage. "Knock yourself out."

I thank him and head for the back of the room. As I reach the cramped one-person cell, Emma Schroeder looks up at me curiously. I introduce myself.

"What do you want?" she asks testily.

"Information."

"Do I look like an encyclopedia?" she says. "Bug off."

"Why did you accuse Virginia Jenks of killing your husband?"

"It felt good. Goodbye."

She turns her back to me. I lean up against the bars and wait. Finally she looks back over her shoulder. "You still here?"

"Still waiting," I say.

"What's your interest?" she asks.

"I have a problem with Virginia Jenks."

She laughs. "Well, don't we all."

"Still waiting," I say.

She hesitates, then nods. "Okay. Last summer Leon walked out on me and moved in with her. I loved him a little, I guess. He was a decent enough meal ticket but still, there was some love in there somewhere. I guess mostly my pride was hurt. I know who and what I am. I'm sexy and I'm pretty and my pride was shattered by this mama's boy. By the way, that was the only good thing about his walkout. I didn't have to deal with his bitch of a mother again."

"Good for you. Now, about her killing him?"

"Yeah. It was right after New Years. Jenks was always bugging him about doing something important with his life, whatever the hell that means. I guess like 'be somebody'. Write a play or a book or even some goddamned poems like she did. Poor Leon, he just liked to coast along, enjoying life, avoiding pressure and here she was busting his balls to turn him into something he wasn't. And then one night, around two in the morning, he supposedly suffered a major heart attack. I say supposedly because no really knows what happened and since there was no autopsy we'll probably never know. Jenks called an ambulance but by the time it arrived, he was gone."

"And you think she killed him."

"All that pressure, day after day, and him with a father who died of a coronary at the age of 31. Yeah, I think she killed him. Not with poison or a pillow over his face, but she might as well have." She hesitates thoughtfully. "Not that I'm totally ruling out poison."

"Discovered no doubt in the autopsy," I say impatiently. I think this woman may be weaving a fairy tale.

"My husband's body lay in the morgue for three days before anyone got around to looking at him. By that time all traces of poison had dissipated or so I was told. I really didn't believe it. I still don't."

"And exactly what kind of poison was it?" I ask.

"The kind that kills people," she says nastily. "How the hell should I know?"

"You've built up a lot of hate over someone you describe as a mama's boy."

"I have. Did I mention the insurance? A nice little policy worth $35,000."

"I'd hardly call that little," I say.

"Just before Christmas he changed the beneficiary from me to her. I'm his wife, for Gods sake. She's... she's what she is. And then suddenly he dies. At his age? You think this is all coincidence?"

I nod. "I can see how you'd be upset that she got the money---"

"No, no. She hasn't got it yet. My lawyer's seen to that. There are laws in this state about community property even she can't get around. No, little Miss Sunshine hasn't got the money yet. The insurance company lawyers and my lawyer are still sorting it out."

She's been looking me in the eye. Now she looks past my shoulder and reacts. "About time," she mutters.

I turn and see a distinguished looking man in his early 30's wearing a camels hair coat talking to Moreno. He nods. Moreno nods and then the two of them start toward us.

"Jesus, Harlow, it took you long enough!" she yells as he nears.

"Sorry," he says, "traffic tie up." He looks at me and puts out his hand. "Harlow Quinn," he says.

"Joe Bernardi."

Meanwhile, Moreno is unlocking the cell and Emma comes out, goes to Quinn with a hug and plants a big one right on his lips. He looks a little embarrassed by this. Probably went to Harvard.

"You're free to go, Mrs. Schroeder," Moreno says. "If Miss Jenks shows up and insists on pressing charges I'll let you know."

"Thanks, Detective," Quinn says.

Moreno shrugs. "Always happy to accomodate the D.A.s office," he says.

Emma and Quinn walk off arm in arm. I watch after them and then glance over at Moreno.

"Assistant D.A.," he says. "The town's full of them. What are you gonna do?"

I take my leave knowing only a little more than I did when I walked in. Frail little Virginia may be something of a ball buster and I warn myself not to be fooled by that waif-like appearance. She has stolen my book. How she did it I don't know but I will find out and I will expose her. Meanwhile I have other priorities. I need to rush home and corner Bunny in the bedroom where I will force her to hustle and tussle with me until midnight or beyond. At ten tomorrow morning she will wing her way eastward and like a prudent squirrel I am going to store up vivid memories, enough to last several days at least.

The following morning I drive Bunny and her three huge fully packed suitcases to Los Angeles International Airport. Last year there was no "International" but L.A. is playing with the big boys now. Predictably Bunny has brought enough clothes to survive six weeks without going near a washing machine. It is mid-May. If New York suddenly suffers prolonged blasts of arctic air that freeze over the lakes in Central Park, she is ready. And if the temperature spikes into the high nineties and every fire hydrant in the five boroughs is wrenched open to provide watery relief, she is ready for that, too. Bunny misses very little and is prepared for everything. Since I am not from Harvard I give her a huge public smooch at the departure gate and watch as she trips gaily out toward the plane. She's a kid getting her first pair of skates, a teenager going on her first date, a young mother holding her first baby in her arms. Bunny is in a world of her own.

Back at the office Glenda Mae is her usual ebullient self. The must-read mail is on my desk along with the Times and the trades. I have two messages. Barry Loeb wants me to call when I get in. Jane Wyman will be in wardrobe after eleven o'clock. Drop by if you get a chance.

I call Barry, hoping for encouraging news. He has none. Quite the opposite.

"Ed North never read your book," he says.

"What?" I say in disbelief.

"That's what I heard from Chaz Lambo over at RKO. North read two or three pages of the first chapter, skimmed through, read a little here and there and decided you were a pretty literate guy and called his friend Robert Wilder who told North he would be delighted to read the manuscript. And as we know, the manuscript got lost in the mail."

"Damn," I mutter.

"North's on vacation in the Bahamas but Chaz gave me a phone number if you want to confirm"

"No, I'll take his word," I say.

"You find out anything about this guy Shelley?" Barry asks.

"Not a he. Virginia Jenks. She tacked on the Shelley because Percy gives her tingles up her spine."

"I don't suppose she mentioned how she happened to come by your book."

"In her own ladylike way, she told me to piss up a rope."

"Ah," Barry says, "not only a thief but literate as well."

I tell Barry I'm not sure what to do next but I think it's going to involve a phone call to Robert Wilder. I say I'll get back to him and I hang up. Time to earn my paycheck and since it's past eleven, I head out toward the wardrobe department. On the way out I ask Glenda Mae to get me a home phone number for Wilder. Could be in New York or Virginia. Maybe check with his publisher. I give her little to go on but I know that within an hour or two I'll have the number. Second only to Bunny, she is the one female I cannot live without.

Jane is sitting on a sofa in the waiting room leafing through the newest issue of 'Photoplay'. Who says stars don't read fan mags? They thrive on them. She looks up with a smile as I enter. We're old pals since 'The Lady Takes a Sailor' which I worked on for several weeks last year getting it prepped for release. It wasn't the happiest time for her. She was in the midst of a divorce from Ronnie Reagan but trouper that she was, she kept her personal problems out of the workplace and we laughed together a lot. She also was only mildly enthused by the picture. It was far from the challenge of 'Johnny Belinda' for which she had won the Oscar earlier in the year. I suspect that Oscar may be the reason she has asked to see me.

"You are looking so wonderful, Joe," she says. "Is there a new lady in your life?"

"Same one," I say, "but she's growing on me. Gonna do my best to hang onto her."

"Good for you," she says. And then she adds with a rueful smile, "I think I'm done. Three marriages and out. Eight years with Ronnie and we still couldn't keep it going."

"Don't quit on yourself, Janie. You're young and beautiful. Who knows what gorgeous hunk of manhood is waiting around the next corner?"

"Thanks, Joe, but from now on it's me and the kids."

"You're disappointing a lot of guys out there."

"They'll get over it," she says. "So, Joe, how do you like the script?"

"For 'Menagerie'? Love it," I say.

"Good script. Good cast. Good part. I think I can do something very special with Laura."

"No doubt about it," I tell her. "The part's made for someone of your caliber."

"Thanks for saying that. I'm a little nervous. But I do know that if I hit the right notes, the performance will be a standout." She's circling now, getting ready to land. "I think it's worth a real publicity push and there's no time like the present to start working on it."

I decide to say it for her. "I agree. With this part I definitely think we are looking at an Oscar nomination."

Her eyes widen and she smiles demurely. "Oh, do you think so, Joe?"

"Absolutely," I say.

She shakes her head. "I dare not think it," she says. "I've already been blessed. I've had my moment. Still---" She hesitates. "Didn't Luise Rainer win two years in a row? I suppose it could happen again."

"I'm sure of it," I say.

At this moment I look past her as a young assistant with safety pins and straight pins adorning her work smock emerges from the back.

"Well, a second Oscar would be lovely but even a nomination would be a thrill. But even if that were not to happen, Joe, we both know it's the work that counts. Everything else is really secondary."

I smile. I've heard that same thing elsewhere. I look at the wardrobe assistant who raises her eyes to heaven. Also something I have recently seen.

I tell Janie I am going right back to my office and start organizing a campaign. She takes my hand and squeezes it and out I go, leaving Janie content and optimistic. I start the short walk back to my office. I think, so far, so good, but can Gertrude Lawrence be far behind?

When I get back to my office, Glenda Mae asks if I'd like to speak with Robert Wilder. She's tracked him down to a phone number in New York supplied by his publisher. It's not clear if this is his residence or a friend's place where he is visiting. I ask her to place the call.

After two rings, a woman answers.

"Hello."

"Hi. I'd like to speak to Mr. Wilder, please."

"Who's calling?"

"Joe Bernardi, Warner Brothers publicity."

"Just a minute."

A moment later Wilder is on the phone. I get a jovial greeting.

"Mr. Bernardi, a delight to talk to you. Ed North says you're one of a kind."

"I take it that's a compliment," I say.

"Most assuredly," he says. He speaks with a soft Virginia accent and sounds a lot like Randolph Scott.

"Well, the feeling is mutual, Mr. Wilder. I enjoyed 'Flamingo Road' from cover to cover. Also 'Written on the Wind'."

"Pleased to hear it," he says. "Universal's talking option on that one."

"Smart. It'll make a good film," I say.

"Sorry about that mixup on your book, Joe. Okay if I call you Joe?"

"Sure."

"Can't figure what happened. I was looking forward to reading it. I get a kick out of finding new writers, especially publicists, having been one myself."

"You're kidding," I say.

"Indeed not. A short time serving Claudette Colbert. A lovely lady who very much adored my work. But as you know, I harbored greater ambitions. Pity she broke her leg and had to give up 'All About Eve'. Davis is good. Claudette would have been better."

"Perhaps so," I temporize. "I suppose you've double checked everywhere my manuscript could be."

"Doubled and tripled. Here. My place in Virginia. My apartment here in New York. My studio in Los Angeles. No sign anywhere. I even put a call in to that fill-in secretary I hired but no luck there either."

"Fill in secretary?" I say alertly.

"Yes. I broke my arm about seven months ago so I needed someone to type manuscript from my dictation. I was hip deep in 'Wait for Tomorrow' which I subsequently finished but at the time I was up against a deadline. He proved to be a life saver."

"You say 'he'." I say.

"Yes, he was a terrific typist, very good proofreader. Very bright. Very organized. I say 'was' because I found out the poor fellow had died a few months ago."

"Do you remember his name?"

"Of course. It was Leon. Leon Schroeder."

CHAPTER SIX

The picture, once murky, is starting to come into focus. Leon Schroeder, working temporarily for novelist Robert Wilder, had access to my book when it arrived in the mail. Thinking perhaps that it was unsolicited and unwelcome, he read a few pages, found it worthwhile and decided to adopt it as his own. Joseph Bernardi? Who the hell was he? Some wannabe writer out of the tens of thousands of wannabe writers who infest the publishing community? And if he confiscates my book, who will know the difference? It's a good book, highly readable. So he changed locales, character names and other small details and put his name on the title page. There was a slight risk he would be unmasked as a plagarist but it was worth the gamble. Now he can be somebody in the eyes of his beloved Virginia.

But then Leon had the bad manners to die and there was Virginia with her lover's brilliant novel on her hands, unread by anyone but her and certainly unpublished. What to do? Leon's dead. No one's going to want to publish a first time novel from a writer who will be unable to write a second so Virginia, ambitious in her own right, re-typed the title page and became an instant novelist, not merely a failed poetess. Does that make sense? It does to me. In spades.

I'm breathing a little more easily now. It'll be simple to show Leon Schroeder's access to my book and the connection to Virginia is obvious. It won't take much to prove my authorship.

I am deep in thought when I hear a knock and look up. Tennessee Williams is standing in my open doorway.

"Busy?"

"Not really."

"I only need a minute."

"Come on in." I say.

He does, pulling up my guest chair. He refuses any kind of refreshment and gets right to the point.

"Frank and I are flying out for the Keys tomorrow morning but I wanted to make sure before I left that we had no misunderstanding."

"About what?"

"Our conversation in the commissary. I had some unkind things to say and I do not like to be thought of as an unkind man."

I interrupt him. "Mr. Williams----"

He wags a finger at me.

"Tom. Remember?"

"Tom," I say. "I understood perfectly that whatever we discussed was off the record. You needn't worry on that account."

He smiles."I am relieved. I should hate to be introduced to Miss Lawrence feeling that she thinks ill of me. More than that, I am told that ths studio is in negotiations for the film rights to "Streetcar". I would not like to bollix that up."

"Understood."

"Excellent," he beams and starts to rise.

"May I ask you something, Tom?" I say.

"Certainly," he says, sitting back down.

"Have you ever had any of your work stolen from you?"

"You mean plagarized?"

"Yes."

"No, I haven't nor would I have permitted it. I have little enough to offer this world. What I have I guard jealously." He cocks his head. "Why? Have you been victimized?"

"I have," I say.

"Do not let it go unchallenged, Joe. Our art is more than mere words, it is the core of our souls. Fight for it."

"I intend to."

"Good man," he says, rising and heading toward the door. He stops and looks back at me. "My apologies, Joe. I lied. On second thought I do remember an occasion when my words were purloined by another. It was my first year at the University of Missouri. I wrote a short piece for my journalism class about the mating habits of badgers. It was supposed to be humorous but I failed miserably and tossed it into the trash. A slowwitted and lazy classmate retrieved it and submitted it to the professor under his own name. As I recall he was rewarded with a D." He smiles. "You see, Joe, justice does exist in this world if only in dribs and drabs." He waves goodbye and is on his way.

Yes. Justice. That's what I'm looking for. Justice and recognition.

My intercom buzzes.

"Yes, Glenda Mae?"

"There's a woman on line one. Emma Schroeder. She said you'd take her call."

I will, I say, and I do.

"Have I caught you at a bad time?" she asks.

"Not at all," I say.

"Well, knowing of your interest in Virginia Jenks, I thought

I would let you know that the District Attorney's office has ordered an exhumation of Leon Schroeder's body."

"Really? Why would they do that?"

"Looking for traces of poison," she says.

"Oh, I see. Murder most foul. And didn't they already do that?"

"I was unsatisfied."

"And what inspired the D.A.'s office to take this sudden and belated action?"

"It's a matter of seeing justice done."

"Spurred on by Assistant District Attorney Harlow Quinn?"

"Don't be snide, Mr. Bernardi. You're making me sorry I called you. I thought you would be interested. Sorry for wasting your time." Click. She has hung up.

Well, she's right about one thing. I am interested. It would never have occurred to me that waif-like Virginia could have committed murder but that was before the more ambitious side of her personality began to evidence itself. Could she have poisoned her lover to get her hands on his book? Was she that desperate to make a reputation for herself. Events were becoming odder and odder.

I realize it's lunchtime so I duck down to the commissary to grab a sandwich to go. While I'm waiting for it to be made I spot my agent, Barry Loeb, lunching with Ruth Roman who is on the lot filming 'Colt .45'. She, too, like Douglas and Kennedy, got a career boost from 'Champion' and I suspect Barry is trying to woo her into signing with the Morris office. Barry catches my eye and quickly excusing himself, he hurries to my side.

"Cute date you've got there, Barry. A woman you can really look up to," I say.

"Will you quit with the short jokes," he says, "or I'll start on your ears."

"Me and Gable," I grin.

"You wish. Listen, I just got it through the jungle drums. RKO has put a temporary hold on the film. They heard about about the business at the coffee house and it's making them nervous."

"Excellent," I say. "And within a few days I will have reclaimed ownership of the property and you can begin negotiating."

He cocks his head uncertainly. "Maybe yes, maybe no. I'll have to check your contract."

"For what?"

"You might have to offer Warners first look."

"Why? They didn't hire me as a screenwriter."

"You'd be surprised the junk they can hide in the small print. I'll call you later this afternoon."

"I'll be around. Have a nice lunch." I smile and wave at Ruth. She smiles and waves back. She has no idea who I am but this is Hollywood. Aspiring actresses smile and wave at everyone.

I go back to my office and eat my BLT, washing it down with a Nehi and then I sit back in my chair and put my brain to work. Often when I do this, I fall asleep but today I am actually able to think cognitively and before long, I have come up with a plan that I believe will prove my authorship beyond doubt. It will require a return trip to the offices of Maybelle Ruskin. I debate whether to call first or rely on surprise. I opt for the latter.

Within the hour I once again find myself climbing the stairs to Maybelle Ruskin's cramped little office on the third floor of the tumbledown building on Highland Avenue. I open the outer door and enter. Again the door to Maybelle's private sanctum is ajar but I hear no strains from Verdi. Instead, Maybelle seems to be in an animated phone conversation with someone named

Olivia. I poke my head in hopefully and Maybelle sees me. She gestures to a small settee against the wall, simultaneously raising her eyes to heaven in obvious frustration.

"Olivia, listen to me. I have no idea what is running through Virginia's mind and even less about that harridan, Emma Schroeder." Pause. "Oh, please. As her sister, you know perfectly well Virginia is incapable of murder. You've been to that rattrap of a bungalow she lives in. Magazines and books piled high to the ceiling and vermin running all over the place because she is too softhearted to set a mousetrap." Pause. "Frankly, Olivia, I do not know what has driven Emma to instigate this exhumation other than old fashioned revenge. You tell your mother that there is no way in hell that Virginia is any danger from this ridiculous waste of time." Pause. "Olivia, you are starting to rant and I haven't the patience for it. I have given you my opinion. I have told you what I know. If you are unsatisfied, speak to Virginia directly." Pause. "Yes, I know. When hell freezes over." Pause. "I'm hanging up now, Olivia. Goodbye." And with that Maybelle disconnects the call.

She looks over at me, shaking her head in visible annoyance. "A dreadful woman. I cannot believe that she is Virginia's sister."

"Didn't know she had one," I say.

Maybelle nods. "Older by two years. Fancies herself an aesthete but there isn't an artistic bone in her body even though she operates an art gallery on Rodeo Drive in Beverly Hills."

"She must be struggling then," I opine.

"No, actually she seems to be doing fairly well. Her clientele is even less art savvy than she is and her slick boyfriend could sell porterhouse steaks to a vegetarian." She reaches into a colorful lacquered box on her desk and withdraws a cigarette which she inserts into the end of a long pink cigarette holder.She lights up and inhales deeply, then lets the smoke out slowly. The process seems to calm her.

"Do you know who I am, Mr. Bernardi?" she asks.

I make a wild stab. "Literary agent and career consultant?" It's posted on her door.

"I am Switzerland," she says. "When two countries detest each other to the point that they cannot even maintain diplomatic relations, they rely on Switzerland to act as a go-between. Virginia is heaven, Olivia is hell and I am Switzerland."

"Fontaine and deHavilland," I mutter under my breath.

"What?"

"Never mind. And what seems to be the root cause of this animosity?" I ask.

"Sibling rivalry honed to a keen edge. That and eight million dollars." She sees I am unaware. "They share a widowed mother who is in the worst of health, bedridden, attended by legions of doctors and nurses and filthy rich. The contents of Lucretia Jenks' last will and testament remain known only to Lucretia and her attorney. As a result enmity reigns." She smiles mirthlessly and takes another long drag on the pink cigarette holder. "But enough of my troubles, Mr. Bernardi. I heard how you came to Virginia's aid the other evening. How may I help you?"

"Well, it's really about how I can help you," I say. "I've been told that RKO has temporarily put Virginia's deal on hold, partly because of the altercation with Emma Schroeder and partly because of my claims to the property."

"You have been told correctly," Maybelle says.

"Well, I feel badly. From what I've gleaned from the screenplay it sure looks like my work, but maybe I'm wrong. Maybe it's a monstrous coincidence. If I could just get a look at Virginia's manuscript maybe we can clear this up."

Maybelle shakes her head, turning her back on me and walking over to the window overlooking the street. "No, no. That's impossible," she says.

I get up and follow her over. I'm going to force her to deal with me, like it or not. "Surely you must have a photostatic copy," I say.

"Of course," she replies, "but I couldn't let it out of my sight."

"Oh, I wouldn't dream of asking you to do that, but I was hoping perhaps you'd let me read a part of it here in your office. It shouldn't take me long to discover if it's my work or not." Maybelle wavers momentarily, trying to process the pros and cons. "If it's not mine it'll certainly relieve my mind and yours, too, Miss Ruskin. We can put all this unpleasantness behind us."

Finally, she nods. "All right, you sit there at the coffee table and read. I'll give you a half hour, no more."

"Excellent," I say, sitting back down on the settee and drawing the coffee table closer.

Maybelle pulls a set of keys from her purse and opens the bottom drawer of her desk. She extracts a box and brings it to the table. I lift the lid. It contains several hundred photostatic sheets. The top one reads,"No Home of My Own" by V.J. Shelley. A perfect hostess, Maybelle offers me coffee while I am reading and I gratefully accept. She moves to the other end of the room where an aluminum percolator sits atop a hot plate. As she pours the coffee into a delicate bone china cup, I grab one sheet of the manuscript from the middle of the pile and in one deft motion, fold it and slip it into my jacket pocket. When she returns with my coffee I am deep into concentration on the first page of the novel.

It takes all my willpower to keep from screaming. My

protagonist is named Walt. He has been changed to Henry. Walt lived with his foster family in a little farmhouse in Nebraska. Henry hails from North Dakota. Character names and places are changed but incidents remain the same. Leon Schroeder was some kind of fool if he thought he could get away with this.

I continue the charade as long as I can without vomiting all over Maybelle's circular hooked rug and then I return the pages to the box and cover it with the lid.

"I may have made a mistake," I say contritely.

Maybelle smiles. "I am so glad," she says, "for both our sakes."

"I'd like to apologize to Virginia in person. Could you tell me where she lives?"

"Oh, no, I couldn't do that," Maybelle says, shocked that I would ask. "Virginia guards her privacy diligently," she says.

"Surely in this case you could make an exception, Miss Ruskin," I say.

"Surely in this case I cannot, Mr. Bernardi," Maybelle responds forcefully. "However, if you wish to express your regrets face to face, tomorrow evening at six, Virginia will again be reciting at The Jabberwocky." Oh, God no, I think. "Later that evening, she will also be reciting at nine o'clock at Vernon's Booketeria a few blocks away."

I smile as I get up from the settee. "Then I will be seeing her tomorrow evening. Thank you for your help and kindness, Miss Ruskin. You make a great Switzerland."

She smiles at that.

By the time I reach my car, I am not feellng very good about myself. Maybelle Ruskin is a very nice woman, a very trusting woman and I have violated that trust. The fact that I had little choice does not console me. That single sheet of manuscript feels like a lead weight in my jacket pocket.

CHAPTER SEVEN

t's pushing six o'clock and normally I'd be on the way home by now but I really have no interest in walking into an empty house, heating up a lousy can of Campbell's chicken noodle soup and watching some mind-numbing television show like that new inanity, Beat The Clock, emceed by the guy who used to play Superman on the radio. He should have stuck to blue tights and his big S.

I go back to the office to check things out and maybe grab a bite at the commissary. My stomach is in a state of rebellion due to lack of food. I also think I might stroll down to sound stage 4 where they are shooting some pick up shots for 'The West Point Story'. Cagney's going to be there along with Ginny Mayo and Doris Day, Gordon MacRae and Gene Nelson. I've been told it's a song and dance scene with Cagney hoofing it. Watching a movie being made is tedious business but watching Cagney do a routine, that's something else.

Glenda Mae is gone for the day but on my desk I find a large manila envelope. I ignore it for the moment while I get the studio operator to place a long distance call for me to the Waldorf Astoria Hotel in New York City, room 344. I know it's unlikely that Bunny will be in. Odds are she is carousing at one of the city's infamous nightclubs, oblivious to the fact that her soulmate is in a wretched state of loneliness. Nonetheless I feel compelled to at least try to get through to her.

As I wait for the operator to get back to me, I turn my attention to the envelope. Inside I find a sheaf of maybe two dozen recipes and a note from Eleanor Parker's husband, Bert. These are old family recipes, he writes, and might be of interest to Good Housekeeping or Redbook or maybe McCall's. He's thinking of a special layout with Eleanor at home cooking for the family with lots of photos to go along with the recipes. Not that Bert wants to tell me how to do my job, just a suggestion off the top of his head. Naturally I am thrilled beyond words. This sort of helpful cooperation is something we publicity flacks look forward to just as we look forward to catching pneumonia when winter sets in.

I put the envelope aside when the phone rings. I pick up quickly. The studio operator tells me there was no answer in the room. The operator says she has left a message that I had called. I thank her and hang up. Still hungry, I decide to amble over to stage 4 and steal supper from the craft services table. But before I can douse the lights, my phone rings. Aha. My beloved has just walked into her room and discovered my call. Best of all, she is not out getting plastered at the Copacabana.

"Hi, cutie. Miss me yet?" I coo into the phone.

"I beg your pardon." Unless Bunny has suddenly developed bronchitis, it's a man's voice.

"Who's this?" I say, slightly embarrassed.

"Is this Joseph Bernardi?" the man asks.

"It is," I say. "And who are you?"

"Well, I'm sure not cutie," he says. "This is Richard Aldrich."

Uh, oh. This is not some encyclopedia salesman. This is Gertrude Lawrence's husband.

"Mr. Aldrich, a pleasure to speak to you. I thought you might have been my lady love."

"So I gathered."

"She's in New York at a convention."

"I see."

"She just left this morning. I had placed a call just to see how she was doing."

"Considerate of you," he says.

"I thought you were her," I say.

"Yes, we covered that," he says.

I realize now that I am boring this guy to tears.

"So, Mr. Aldrich, how may I help you?"

"Well," he says, "Gert and I are in town just for tonight and seeing that we all will be working together soon, she wondered if you might join us tonight for dinner. I realize it's late and you may have other plans----"

"As a matter of fact I don't and I'd be delighted," I say.

"Excellent. Shall we say Scandia's at nine o'clock?"

"Perfect," I say as my stomach continues to gurgle.

"Do you know how to get there?" Aldrich asks.

"Who doesn't?" I laugh cavalierly as if I dine there thrice a week.

When I hang up I realize I will never make it to nine o'clock so I start wolfing down peanuts from my emergency jar on the shelf. In my opinion nine o'clock dinners are for barbarians.

The restaurant, which has become a favorite of L.A.'s elite in the four years it has been open, is located in the 9000 block of Sunset Boulevard. The valet accepts my unwashed Ford without a whimper and stashes it between a Ferrari and a Porsche. When I walk in I am taken slightly aback by the decor which seems to consist mainly of colorful coats of arms, all historically Danish. No Galahad, no Lancelot and no round table. The parts of the walls that are not masked by family crests are elegant panels of dark wood from which are hung a variety of copper and brass fixtures.

I spot the two of them immediately sitting at a decent sized table in the middle of the room where they can see and be seen. She is elegantly dressed in cream-colored satin set off by a ruby necklace and matching earrings. It is not a dress so much as a gown and she is perfectly dressed for a Presidential ball. He is wearing a midnight blue tuxedo with a cummerbund and bow tie in matching yellow plaid. I am aware that my top of the line Brooks Brothers suit and Countess Mara tie do not measure up.

As I approach the table Aldrich stands to greet me and Gertrude throws me a hundred guinea smile designed to melt away any reservations I may now have or will ever have about the darling of London's West End. Aldrich and I shake hands. Gertrude extends her hand and I air-kiss her finger tips. Greetings done with, I sit and quickly look her over. At 52 she is a strikingly handsome woman with an excellent figure. I suspect she works hard to keep it that way.

"How about a drink, Joe?" Aldrich says, signaling our waiter.

"Sure," I say. "Coors beer."

"Not here, I'm afraid," Aldrich tells me. "Bring our guest a Carlsberg," he tells the waiter. Obviously I have no say in the matter.

"I do so love this place, don't you, Mr. Bernardi?" Gertrude is saying to me.

"Nothing like it in the world," I say. "So, your husband tells me you will be in town just for the evening, Miss Lawrence."

"Yes, a pity. I do so love Los Angeles. But I am afraid I am a slave to my public. After I sign my contract with the studio tomorrow morning, I am winging off to San Francisco to meet with Charles Laughton who is planning to stage a reading of Shaw's 'Don Juan in Hell' next year on Broadway. The dear man insists I must be a part of his production."

"Fascinating," I say, totally at sea. Is she talking George Bernard or Irwin because I have never heard of this Don Juan thing.

"And then Noel insists we visit him in Aruba and of course, we are terribly excited. We haven't seen him in nearly a year," she continues.

At that moment the waiter comes to the table with my beer and then, having delivered it, stands back, pen poised as he looks down at me expectantly.

"Gert and I have already ordered, Joe." Aldrich says. "We always have the same thing, you know. Lammersaddel for two, lamb roasted and carved at the table. However, I can recommend anything on the menu. It's all first rate."

I glance at the menu which fortunately explains in English what I am getting into. I quickly settle on the Dansk Hakke Bof which sounds strangely like a hamburger. When it comes I am delighted to see that it IS a hamburger.

We chat amiably over drinks and through the salad course until finally Aldrich gets to the point of this meal. As if I couldn't guess. He's a little like Eleanor Parker's husband Bert but with a soupcon more suavity.

"Gert is very excited about the role of Amanda. Very unlike anything she's ever done," he says.

"A monumental challenge," she says. "I'm absolutely thrilled by it. So well written, so well defined. When Mr. Warner personally called to ask me to participate, I was flattered beyond words. Of course I am not thrilled by my billing but this is my problem, Mr. Bernardi, not yours."

Aldrich smiles. "This is a major opportunity for Gert to connect with the American movie going public. She's made very few films, you know."

"Nine, darling," she says, "but this will be my first all-American movie with an all-American cast. I plan to work very, very hard, Mr. Bernardi, to make it an artistic as well as a commercial success."

"Your participation practically guarantees it, Miss Lawrence," I say.

"You are a dear. Thank you. And I'm sure you can understand when I say that an all out publicity campaign that highlights this participation can only enhance the regard in which the film will be held."

"I will make it a priority," I say.

"Of course you will," Aldrich smiles. "Gert is already the first lady of London theater. Her success on Broadway is without parallel. And now we must make her a household name with moviegoers all across this wonderful country."

"And naturally you will have my full cooperation, Mr. Bernardi," Gertrude says. "Merely ask and I will make myself available. I ask only that you keep me apprised of any and all publicity your office generates. It needn't be detailed. A one or two page memo every week should suffice."

Aldrich chimes in as I look from one to another. "And if all goes well, a few months from now, I expect that there will be well-deserved talk of an award for Gert's performance, that's how enthused we both are over the prospects for this project."

Gertrude nods. "Not that an award would be the only measure of my contribution. After all, the work itself will be its own reward, but if an Academy Award should come my way, well, wouldn't that be the perfect recognition of a job well done? The cherry atop the sundae, as they say."

Indeed, it would, I think to myself, wondering whether a sheaf of recipes can be far behind.

That night I do not sleep well. Maybe it was the Dansk Hakke Bof which was a hamburger with secret ingredients, all perfectly digestible by the Danes. Unfortunately, I am Italian. Or maybe it wasn't the meal, maybe it was the fact that every time I threw my arm across the bed to draw Bunny close, she wasn't there. I try hot tea and milk, then hot milk without the tea. Nothing works. I stare wide-eyed at the ceiling. I am perilously close to becoming an old married man who cannot survive without his mate.

Bleary-eyed I get into the studio at nine. Gertrude will be in Jack Warner's office at ten for the official signing of the contract and my ace photographer, Buddy Raskin, will be there to memorialize it. Then and only then will I be able to tell the world of our coup, messengering out the release and photo to the local press. Despite this there is always someone who wants to jump the gun and in this case it's my pal Phineas Ogilvy from the Times who has learned of my dinner date with the Aldriches the night before. Phineas is a true character, a flamboyant self-made celebrity, often more interesting than the people he writes about. In a battle of wits you have lost before you open your mouth but for all his pretensions, Phineas is a genuinely nice and caring person, a trait he manages to disguise most of the time. Now he has cleverly put two and two together but I cannot confirm his suspicions. Only a fool releases this kind of a story before the ink is dry on the contract. Phineas grudgingly agrees to wait for official confirmation.

I'm drinking coffee and leafing through my mail, glancing at my wall clock every minute or two and wondering why the day is passing so slowly. I am mildly annoyed with Bunny who has yet to get back to me and I am beginning to wonder why. I'm sure that if she had some sort of problem she'd call me. Maybe there is no problem. Maybe she's just having a helluva good time and I am an afterthought if I am any kind of thought at all. I vow not to let it get to me. First things first. Tonight's the night I get my life back and it can't come soon enough. I am a man with a plan and nothing is going to get in the way of it.

There's a gentle tap on my door jamb and I look up. Janie Wyman is peering in. "Did I catch you at a bad time?" she asks.

I smile and wave her in. I always have time for Janie. She's one of my favorites. I point to a chair but she shakes her head. She's busy this morning. She only has a minute.

"I'm flying off to St. Joe tomorrow morning," she tells me. "My alma mater, Lafayette High School, is planning a tribute in my honor with a showing of 'Johnny Belinda'. Obviously I'm flattered and very excited."

Who can blame her, I think, although I'm not so sure about the alma mater part since I know for a fact that she dropped out of high school when she was 15 years old.

"They tell me the local papers will be covering the event with lots of photos which, naturally, I have asked them to forward on to you."

"Good thinking."

"If you get a chance, you might want to call the local editors with some suggestions on maximizing coverage." She reaches into her purse and takes out a sheet of paper. "I took the liberty of getting their names and phone numbers. I hope you don't mind."

"Why should I mind?" I smile.

She smiles back and sits down in the chair I had just offered her.

"After St. Joe, I thought I would fly into Ocala, Florida. It's right next to the Juniper Prairie Wilderness where we shot 'The

Yearling' five years ago. The mayor and the city council were delighted I was coming and have arranged some sort of tribute. I thought you should know."

"Excellent," I say. "I'll follow up immediately."

"You see the synergy, don't you, Joe? Back to the scene of my first Oscar nomination and looking forward to perhaps another."

I nod. I get it. Meanwhile she has pulled another sheet of paper from her purse. This one has the name of the mayor and his home phone number. Janie now looks like she's settled in for the morning and I wonder if she may not be missing some sort of beauty appointment.

"Oh, and there's one other thing, as long as I'm in the neighborhood, I understand that Mr. Williams has an apartment in New Orleans and it might be helpful if you could arrange a meeting between the two of us to discuss the upcoming film. We might even be able to squeeze in a radio interview." She digs back into her purse. "There are three major stations in New Orleans. I was able to get the names of the station managers." Smiling, she hands me another sheet of paper.

This is the first I've heard that central Florida and southern Louisiana are neighbors but I let it go. Who am I to mute Janie's enthusiasm? I wonder what other tricks she's hiding in that handbag but no, she seems to be done for the day.

She stands, ready to leave. I stand, thanking her again for all her help. She smiles.

"This is fun, isn't it, Joe?"

I allow as how it is and she leaves. I sag back into my chair. It is mid-May. Oscar campaigning doesn't start in earnest until after Labor Day. Nomination voting doesn't close until after the first of the year and the awards won't be handed out until March

21, 1951.That is ten months from now. These threaten to be the longest ten months of my life.

My day's work done by five o'clock and against my better instincts, I decide to give Bunny one more call. I am rewarded when the phone is answered on the first ring. The downside is, the voice on the line isn't Bunny's. It's a guy.

"Bunny's room," he says.

"Who's this?" I ask.

"Who's this?" he asks back.

"This is Joe," I say.

"Nice to finally talk to you, Joe. This is Walter."

Walter. Wonderful. Who the hell is Walter?

"Bunny wanted to get back to you last night but it was too darned late. Can you believe we were sitting here at two in the morning having dinner?" There's a long pause and then he says, "You have no idea who I am, do you?"

"Matter of fact, I don't."

"Walter Davenport. Editor in Chief of Collier's Magazine. I've sort of taken Bunny under my wing but trust me, Joe, my interest in your lady is strictly professional."

I'm relieved, I think, except that it bothers me that this guy seems to be living in Bunny's hotel room. Does he not have a room of his own?

"Is she there?" I ask.

"Sure," he says jovially. "She's in the tub. I'll get her."

"No!!!" I say, perhaps a little too forcefully. "Tell her I called. I'll try again later."

"You sure, Joe? No bother to get her," he says.

"Don't trouble yourself, Walt. Later'll be fine."

I hang up. As if I don't have enough on my mind, now I have Bunny to worry about. Not that I know much about the publishing business, but I'm pretty good at mathematical equations. Powerful producer is to struggling, ambitious starlet as influential national editor is to wide-eyed neophyte reporter who is in New York for maybe the first time in her life and is possible prey to anything in an Abercrombie & Fitch suit that smells like Old Spice and printer's ink. Yeah, I think my analogy is pretty good. I'll check it out later, say around midnight which will be three a.m. New York time and an hour at which Walter Davenport should be holed up in his own room, not hers.

I turn my attention to the business at hand. At five-thirty I find myself parked across the street from The Jabberwocky, awaiting the arrival of Virginia Jenks. I am wearing dark glasses and an Irish cap pulled low over my forehead. I do not wish to be recognized, lest my brilliantly conceived plan fall apart. At ten minutes to six, a spiffy new 4-door custom sedan DeSoto drives up and double-parks in front of the coffee house. This is a car I have seen before in the Metro Division parking lot.

There is one empty spot in front of the coffee house blocked off with orange pylons and in a flash, Bahadur Singh has emerged to remove them so the DeSoto can park legally. He waits and then escorts Virginia inside. Interestingly, she has been driven here by the lady with the silly straw hat who joins her as she goes inside. I, on the other hand, do not go inside. The brief sample of Miss Jenks' talent I had previously endured was more than I ever hoped to hear.

I had planned to stay with the car until she emerged after the reading but the presence of the straw hat lady has piqued my curiosity.

Armed with paper and pencil I cross the street and jot down the plate number of her car. I look around and spot a telephone booth nearby. I call my good friend, Mick Clausen, the bail bondsman who is now married to my ex-wife Lydia and ask a favor. I need a name and address to go with the plate number and Mick, who is wise in the ways of Los Angeles officialdom, happily agrees. He says it will have to be tomorrow as the Motor Vehicle offices are now closed. I tell him no problem. I thank him and hang up. I amble back to my car, checking my watch. Quarter past. It'll be at least another forty-five minutes before Virginia takes her final bow. Maybe longer. I don't place a bet on shorter.

Bored to tears, I risk the car battery by turning on the radio to 'Our Miss Brooks' with my favorite English teacher, Eve Arden. I'm a hit or miss listener, mostly because of that irritating twerp Richard Crenna playing a brain dead teen who sounds like fingernails on a blackboard. Someone told me Crenna has ambitions to be a movie star to which I reply, hah! Maybe when pigs fly. Maybe not even then.

Cramped behind the wheel with my eyes starting to close, I almost miss them. My watch says 7:09 when Virginia and the straw hat come out and get back into the DeSoto. After the old lady pulls out and starts down the street, I make a u-turn and follow at a discreet distance. It goes like this for about ten minutes as the DeSoto hits West Hollywood and then turns onto Sunset Boulevard, continuing until it reaches Crescent Heights and turns into the entrance for the Garden of Allah. Wow. I've heard of this place, of course. Synonymous with old Hollywood, it was originally a mansion built over 30 years ago and then developed as an apartment complex by the dancer Alla Nazimova who added twenty-five bungalows in the mid '20s. Anyone who was anyone has stayed here including literary giants like Scott Fitzgerald, Robert Benchley, Ernest Hemingway, Dorothy Parker and George S. Kaufman. Its history also boasts its share of actors and directors but I suspect it was its literary cachet that attracted Virginia to this legendary site. A one time home of giants, she had to be a part of it.

The DeSoto stops at the entrance to the main building and Virginia and the woman get out. They chat for a moment and then embrace warmly. Then the old lady gets back in the car and heads back toward me and then onto Sunset. I duck my head down so I won't be seen and then I drive in and pull into a spot in the parking lot. Virginia is still standing outside the main building chatting with an older gentleman in a three piece suit and a jaunty black derby. They share a laugh and then Virginia turns and instead of entering the building she starts down a pathway that leads to one of the sections of bungalows.

Quickly I exit the car. I don't want her to see me but I must learn which unit is hers, otherwise all of this is for naught. I don't run but I move briskly and when I pass the old gentleman, I smile in greeting as if I belong here. He smiles back. I think I know his face but I can't be sure. An actor from the silent days perhaps. I round the corner. She is just entering the next to last unit on the left hand side. Satisfied I turn around and return to my car. I'm in for at least another hour of waiting. Her engagement at the "booketeria" doesn't start until nine o'clock.

By eight thirty it's turning dark. By eight-forty I'm starting to get nervous. Was her performance cancelled at the last minute or did Maybelle give me the wrong day? A cab pulls into the complex and stops in front of the main building. A minute or so later, Virginia appears from the adjacent pathway and gets into the cab. I watch as it exits the premises but I do not follow. My business is with the next to last bungalow on the left.

In my pocket I have a set of lock picks. I used to be pretty good with them. After a lesson from Mick Clausen I am VERY good. I step up to Virginia's door, look around to make sure I am unobserved and insert the picks. Within twelve seconds the door is open and I am inside. Thoughtfully she has left a table lamp on. I walk around the living room and pull the shades on all the windows, then flip on the overhead light.

Virginia Jenks may be bright though I have yet to be convinced but one thing that she is not is tidy. There are newspapers and magazines piled all over the place. Boxes of god-knows-what are stacked in the corners. A plate with remnants of a spaghetti dinner sits on a small table by a window. Three blankets are casually tossed across the sofa. A wicker basket filled with clothes sits just inside the door to the kitchen. Dust is everywhere and it's obvious the windows need a good washing. Other than that, Good Housekeeping would approve.

I do not immediately see what I am looking for so I start a search. I begin with the boxes in the corner and move on to the coat closet by the doorway. There are no coats but several boxes of books.

It takes me almost twenty minutes but I finally discover it in the bottom of the closet in the laundry room under a giant box of Rinso. As I suspected from my photostat it's a standard desk top Royal. I lift it up and take it into the small kitchen and place it on the table. Then I rummage around for typing paper which I find in a drawer in a desk in the living room. I roll the blank sheet into the platen and then take out my ill-gotten photostat. I check out the first sentence and then type it onto the paper.

"Henry felt the nausea welling up in his chest. The man's head was canted at a strange angle and the smell of death was all around."

Now here's the thing about older, much used used typewriters. No two are alike. Even the same makes and models may have infinitesimal differences, often not visible to the naked eye. Sometimes the differences are glaring. I get lucky. There's a whole lot of glaring going on with this typewriter. For one thing the right hand top of the small "t" is missing. The lower case "e" hits the paper slightly below the rest of the lower case letters. And the capital H is missing a serif on the right hand side. Now I have my proof that my novel was retyped on this particular typewriter by Leon Schroeder who had access to my novel when he was working temporarily for Robert Wilder.

But even as I am congratulating myself on my superlative detective work, I hear voices immediately outside the front door. A woman and a man and I am pretty sure that the woman is Virginia Jenks. What the hell? It's only nine-thirty. What happened to her reading at the booketeria? I don't panic. I snatch up the typewriter and stick it in the bottom of the broom closet. I hear her key in the door. I'm out of time. I dash into the bedroom just as the front door opens and she enters.

"This is odd," I hear her say. "I never leave the overhead light on."

A man says, "Maybe you were distracted".

"And the shades are drawn. That's not like me," she says. "I think someone's been here."

"Would you like me to look around?" he asks.

"I'd be ever so grateful," she says.

I have seconds to save myself. I hit the floor and roll under the bed just as the door opens. From my vantage point looking over a month's collection of dust bunnies, I can see the bottom of a man's trousers and a pair of highly polished shoes. I hold my breath, freeze my muscles and watch as he walks to the closet and pulls the door open. I hear the rustle of clothing and then he shuts the door and walks out of the room.

"No one," he says. "If there was anyone, they are long gone by now. Would you like me to call the police?"

"No."

"Are you sure?"

"And what would I tell them? No, leave it be."

"If you say so."

"Thank you, Oswald. I don't know what I would do without you?"

"You would survive, child. There is steel in your backbone."

"Good night and thank you again," she says.

"As always, my infinite pleasure," he says and I hear him leave.

I assume she is at the door with him. Now is my chance to escape, my only chance. I remember seeing a window at the far end of the room and I must act at once. I roll out from under the bed, take three long loping strides to the window, grab it and start to tug it open. It refuses to budge. I strain. Nothing. I look more closely. Some fool has painted the window shut. I hear a door open.

"What are you doing in my bedroom?" I hear her say in an angry voice. I turn and face her. Virginia Jenks is glaring at me as she tightly grips a pair of sharp looking shears.

CHAPTER EIGHT

I raise my hands defensively.

"Please. Put down the scissors. I'm not here to hurt you," I say.

She raises the shears high, disbelieving me.

"I know you. You're the man who claims I stole his book."

"That's right and that's what I'm doing here."

"Get out!" she hisses. She's angry but there is also fear in her voice and I don't think it's fear of me, I think it's fear of what I have come for.

"No. I'm not leaving. Not until we settle this." I start moving slowly toward her. She backs away.

"I'll call the police," she threatens.

"Please do," I say, folding my arms across my chest. "I'll be glad to wait."

It's not the response she expected and she is momentarily confused. I reach for the shears but when I do she slashes out with them and catches me on the side of the neck. I feel the pain and I know I am cut. I have my hand around her wrist now, trying to wrest the shears from her grasp. She's stronger than she looks. Maybe her adrenalin is kicking in. She fights like a tigress as I try to subdue her and in the process the handle end of the shears catches her hard on the side of her face by her eye. She gasps in pain and in that moment I take the shears from her. She puts her hand to her face and backs away. She looks up at me like a wounded animal.

"If you want to call the police, Miss Jenks, go right ahead but I plan to prove to you, and to them if they are summoned, that the book you claim you wrote is nothing of the sort."

"I just want you to leave," she whines.

"And I will. In a few minutes." My neck is hurting badly. I reach up and touch the wound. When I pull my hand away there is blood on my fingers.

"What do you want from me?"

"Come in the kitchen and I'll show you."

I walk past her into the kitchen. I grab a paper napkin from the counter to stanch the flow of blood, then retrieve the typewriter from the bottom of the broom closet and set it on the small dinette set table. She appears, watching me closely.

"Come in," I say. "I'm not going to hurt you."

She approaches. I go to the desk drawer and take out a sheet of paper and lay it next to the typewriter.

"I want you to type something for me," I say.

"I can't," she says. Then, quickly, "I won't."

"Which is it? Can't or won't?" I ask.

She glares at me, then picks up the sheet and fumbling, places it behind the platen and rolls it into place. It is slightly askew. She makes no move to adjust it. She looks at me expectantly.

"The quick brown fox," I say.

"What?"

"The quick brown fox," I say. "Type it."

She hesitates, then scans the keyboard. She finds the T and punches it. A small "t".

"Sentences start with capital letters," I tell her.

She glares at me and turns her attention back to the keyboard. It takes her a while but she finally finds the cap key. She presses it down and hits the T again. This time she gets a capital T. I wait. She scans. She locates the "h" and hits it. More scanning. She finds the "e". She punches the key.

"How long did it take you to type this manuscript, Virginia? To the nearest year."

"It's not your book," she says angrily.

"Well, we know for sure it isn't yours," I say. "The only thing you typed was a new title page and it probably took you an entire morning."

She says nothing. Then she steps away from the typewriter and sits on one of the kitchen chairs. There's a red welt forming next to her eye and soon it will turn black and blue.

"I know what you think, Virginia. You think this novel was written by your lover, Leon Schroeder, and since he was dead, you saw nothing wrong with appropriating it as your own. But it wasn't his. I wrote it. Every word and when I sent it to Robert Wilder for his criticism, Leon confiscated it and when his work assignment was over, he came back here and unknown to you, changed some names and places, retyped the manuscript and then presented it to you as his own work. He needed to do it, Virginia. To please you and to keep your love and to earn your respect. That's what happened. You can try to believe otherwise but what I have told you is the truth."

Her hands are clasped in front of her and she is staring at them.

"Oh, God, I am so ashamed," she says.

"No need to be," I tell her.

Finally she lifts her head and looks at me. "No publisher

would take on a first novel from a dead author, even I knew that. But the world needed to read this work. Under my name, I thought I might find a home for it. I swear to you I had no idea that Leon hadn't written it. You must believe me."

"I believe you, Virginia. And I understand why you did what you did. But now it's time for you to set things right."

"Yes," she nods.

"I suggest that tomorrow morning you go to see Maybelle Ruskin. Tell her the whole story. Omit nothing. Let her deal with RKO and the publisher."

"All right," she says quietly. Suddenly she grimaces and grabs her stomach.

"Are you okay?" I ask.

"It's nothing," she says. "Peptic ulcer. I worry too much. Can't help it."

"Is there anything I can do?" I offer.

"No. It'll stop."

I squat down beside her and take her hand. "Look, Virginia, what you did, you did for love. I see no evil in you, no malice. This came about because of your love for Leon and his love for you. It is a painful life lesson but no more than that. Put it behind you and get on with your poetry."

"I will," she says.

I rise, pulling her up with me. "I'll be going now," I say, "but don't forget, first thing in the morning. Maybelle."

"I'll remember," she says as we walk through the living room to the front door. I open it and smile at her. She smiles back even though I can see the ulcer is still bothering her.

"It really is a wonderful book, Mr. Bernardi. You have every right to be proud of it."

"Thank you," I say as I start out. Then I stop. "By the way

who was the lady who dropped you off here earlier this evening?"

She smiles sadly. "She was going to be my mother in law," she says.

"Leon's mother," I say.

She nods. "This is going to hit her very hard. Outside of me she was the only one who knew that Leon had written a novel." She shakes her head. "Sorry, you know what I mean."

"I do. It's all right." I think on that for a moment. "So aside from me, she's the only one who knows you took over the book."

"Yes, and she was okay with it. She just wanted to see it published."

I nod and again, wish her luck. The door closes behind me and I hear a click as she turns the lock. I walk down the pathway past the other bungalows, most of which are occupied. I hear a man and a woman arguing. From another bungalow I hear a baby crying. From another a television set blaring loudly enough to awaken Alla Nazimova. I feel vaguely uncomfortable. The grassy areas need mowing and flower beds are lying fallow. There are obvious cracks in the cement walkways and even in the dim light I can see that the little buildings are in need of a paint job. I wonder if Errol Flynn and Cary Grant, once former tenants, would be so willing to settle in given the current state of disrepair. I think not.

I turn the corner and head toward the parking lot feeling good about everything that's transpired. By tomorrow the truth will be known and Barry can go to work finding a home for my novel.

"Hold it right there," I hear him say. "Don't move."

I hear the ominous click of a revolver being cocked and I turn in the direction of the voice which I recognize from Virginia's bungalow. It's almost dark but I can see in the lights from the building that it's the old man she was talking to earlier in the evening and he's holding a pistol aimed directly at my heart. Although I'd put his age at least at 70 and maybe even 80, his grip is steady and his hand doesn't waver.

"Aren't you a little on in years for this sort of thing, old timer?" I say, half raising my hands.

"This isn't a stickup, Mr. Bernardi, and you can lower your hands. I'm quick and I don't miss, in case you decide to try something."

"You know who I am," I say.

"I searched your car. An old library card was in your glove compartment along with a couple of letters addressed to you at Warner Brothers."

"I locked the car," I say.

"So you did," the man says, half smiling.

"You seem to be a man of many talents, Mr. uh----"

"Oswald Pennybaker, former chief of the Ukiah police department, retired nearly twenty years now and yes, I have a permit to carry."

I nod. "And you are holding me up, why? Your pension ran dry? Something like that. "

"We're waiting, Mr. Bernardi."

"For what?"

"Backup," he says.

It is then that I hear the siren and see the flashing lights as a metro police cruiser drives onto the property and pulls to a stop a few feet away.

"I saw your foot sticking out from under the bed but at age 83 with a bum ticker and chronic arthritis I do not face my quarry mano a mano which is why I left to call the authorities and get my firearm. I hope in the interim you did nothing to harm that young woman."

"I didn't. She's fine," I tell him.

"I was fairly sure she would be. You hardly seem the killer type."

The two cops from the cruiser approach, guns drawn.

"I'm Pennybaker," Oswald says. "I'm the one who called."

"Slowly put the gun on the ground, sir," the older of the two cops orders. Oswald complies. "Okay, now what's going on?"

Oswald explains. "A short time ago I escorted the young lady in number 23 to her door. As soon as she opened it, she knew something was wrong. At her request I looked around and spotted this man hiding under the bed. At my age I do not confront anyone so I left her alone and went to call you and to arm myself. I was returning to her bungalow when this man appeared, apparently leaving the premises. I stopped him. A few moments later, you gentlemen arrived."

At this point the second cop has picked up Oswald's gun and is checking it out, sniffing the barrel and examining the cylinder. "Looks like a .38, Manny. Hasn't been fired. Kinda old looking."

"Let me see," the older cops says. He looks it over. "Colt Special. Maybe fifteen or twenty years old," he says.

"Twenty-eight, actually, and I have a carry permit," Oswald says.

Manny the cop looks at me. "What's your story?" he asks.

"It's long and boring," I say.

"I'm a patient guy," Manny says.

Oswald interrupts. "Officer, don't you think we ought to check on the young lady before we do anything else?"

"Good idea," he says. "Show me."

The four of us head down the pathway to number 23. The shades are still drawn but light shows through the cracks and edges. Oswald knocks on the door. There is no response. He knocks again, more loudly. Still no answer. He calls out. "Virginia, it's Oswald!" Nothing. He looks at Manny, concerned.

"We could kick it in," the younger cop says. He looks like the kick-it-in type.

"Get the manager," Manny says.

"No need," Oswald says. He reaches for his wallet and takes out a small plastic card of some kind which he slips into the door crack. He waggles it slightly near the door handle and then twists the handle and pushes the door open.

"What the hell did you just do?" Manny asks.

Oswald holds up the little piece of plastic. I see the words 'Diner's Club' on it. "I got this about four weeks ago. Brand new. It's called a charge card. Also ideal for jimmying doors."

Manny nods appreciatively.

We go inside. As we do we see her immediately. She is lying sprawled on the living room floor and she is very, very still. Deathly still and her face is contorted in pain. My stomach starts to churn and I can feel the bile rising toward my throat. I close my eyes for a moment but when I re-open them nothing has changed. Twenty minutes ago this frail and gentle young woman was full of life and starting to feel good about herself. No more.

Oswald moves quickly to her side, takes her wrist momentarily, the reaches toward her neck and places the back of his hand against her carotid artery.

"There's a pulse. Very faint," he says.

Manny turns to his partner. "Radio for an ambulance!" The youngster hurries from the room as I cross to the living room window that faces out onto the walkway. I try to open it but like the window in the bedroom, coats of of paint have sealed it shut. Manny looks over at me. In the bright light of the living room, he notices the cut on my neck.

"What happened?" he asks pointing to his own neck.

"She swiped at me with a pair of shears," I say.

Manny looks around and sees the shears lying on the floor near the entrance to the kitchen. He moves to them, looks them over and then using a handkerchief, gingerly picks them up. They have blood on them. My blood. He wraps them in the handkerchief and sets them down on a table. Meanwhile I have checked the other doors and windows in the bungalow. Rear door, locked. Other windows, either locked or sealed shut. I go back into the living room.

Manny has knelt down next to Virginia who is unconscious but still clinging to life. He takes a close look at the burgeoning bruise by her eye and looks up at me.

"You do that?"

"We were struggling for the shears," I say. "It was accidental."

Manny nods. Gently he turns her head a couple of inches to reveal blood on the side of her head. He leans in for a closer look, then scans the room. His eyes fall on the nearby coffee table and he gets to his feet. He kneels by the edge of the table and peers closely at the sharp edged corner. The mahogany is dark but now even I can see it. A blood stain.

I look back toward Virginia. Oswald is holding her hand. Now he leans in close, troubled. Again he uses the back of his hand to search for the carotid. Seconds pass. Then slowly he gets to his feet.

"She's gone," he says.

Manny gives me a look and then he walks over to the phone

on the desk and dials a number. "Berg, Emanuel. Badge 1055. We need a unit at the Garden of Allah. Unit 23. Coroner. Forensics. Detective unit. Deceased female. Possible homicide. Cancel the ambulance." He hangs up and looks back at me.

"Stick around. When we're through here, someone from homicide is going to want to hear your long boring story."

"Am I under arrest?" I ask.

"Not yet," Manny replies.

CHAPTER NINE

They've taken me to the Hollywood Division headquarters on N. Wilcox Avenue and parked me in one of those comfy rooms with an oak table, a couple of straight backed chairs and a huge panoramic mirror in case you want to check your hair comb or your face for pimples. Nobody has to tell me that on the other side of the glass are a half dozen voyeurs and peeping Toms waiting for me to confess to any infraction of the Los Angeles penal code. If I do it's win-win all the way around with the arresting cops getting credit for a collar, the city getting primed for the payment of a big fine, and a bail bondsman set to pick up a few bucks worth of easy money. The only loser in this drama would be me so I determine that I will either keep my mouth shut or tell the truth, the whole truth and nothing but the truth.

The detective's name is Califano and he exudes the kind of world weariness you only find in public servants a few scant months away from collecting their pension. He has tousled grey hair, getting thin in front as his forehead attempts to march to the back of his neck. He's in his shirt sleeves, collar open, tie pulled down and indelible stains on his shirt front that even Clorox can't get rid of. His pants were pressed over a week ago, if at all, and his belt has been let out to the furthest hole which isn't quite far enough. My guess is he's divorced. Cops are notorious for screwing up their marriages. Califano seems like no exception.

I tell him my story twice, omitting no detail. If he finds it fascinating, he gives no sign. He says "uh-huh" a lot and scribbles occasionally on a pad of lined yellow paper. When I finish the second time around, he looks at his pad for a long time, trying to piece it together.

"So this guy Schroeder steals your book," he says.

"Yes."

"So you must have been plenty pissed at him."

"No. I never knew him."

He nods tentatively, still staring at his yellow pad.

"So this woman steals the book from Schroeder."

"Yes. After he's dead."

"So you must have been really pissed at this woman," he says.

"I was upset with her, sure."

"Upset enough to slug her so she falls and slams her head on the coffee table and dies?"

I glare at him. "I didn't slug her, she didn't fall and she didn't hit her head. When I left her bungalow she was standing by the door, alive."

"Uh-huh," he says.

"Did you not talk to someone—anyone—who saw me leave while she was standing in the doorway?" I ask in frustration.

He ignores my question. Either that or he's as deaf as a rolling pin.

"She stabs you in the neck with a deadly weapon and you do nothing about it."

"She didn't stab me, she was holding some shears and it was an accidental cut as I tried to get the shears away from her."

"Uh-huh," he says.

Look," I say, "I'm getting awfully tired of 'uh-huh'. Am I under arrest because if I'm not I'm leaving."

"What's your hurry?" he asks.

"It's past midnight. I'm tired and I need sleep and I want to go home." I tell him.

He looks at me, gimlet-eyed. "I know it's past midnight and I, too, am tired and I need sleep and at my house is my daughter and my son-in-law and a three month old baby who cries all night and I DON'T want to go home. Where were we?"

"You were saying 'uh-huh'."

At this moment the door opens and a familiar figure wades in. Aaron Kleinschmidt is a homicide detective assigned to the Metro Division and three years ago he tried to frame me for murder. Since then our relationship has improved and while I would not exactly call him a friend, he no longer considers me to be an ax murderer or some other threat to civilized society. If you were to ask him, he would describe me as an amiable doofus who couldn't find his way around a baseball diamond in broad daylight.

"How ya doin', Angie?" he says to Califano.

"Okay, Aaron. How's by you?"

"Hanging in," he says before glancing over at me. "You're wasting your time with this bird," he says.

"You think so?"

"I've been watching. He's not smart enough to make up a story that stupid. Give me a couple of minutes with him."

Califano shrugs. "Sure. Why not? I can use a break. If you get a confession, make sure he signs it." He gets up and walks out, closing the door. I look at Kleinschmidt. Kleinschmidt looks at me.

"You're getting to be a habit," he says.

"Forty Second Street. 1932. Sung by Bebe Daniels," I say.

"Always the wiseguy."

"You keep setting me up, Sarge."

"Everywhere you go, dead bodies. Smart people should stay away from you."

"They do. In droves," I say. "So, I see we have a new Chief of Police. Same guy you were talking about last year?"

He nods. "Bill Parker. The guy's top of the line, Joe, and smart as hell. He's cleaning out Chief Horrall's deadwood with a shovel."

"Are you going to be okay?" I ask him.

"Yeah, I'm fine," he says. "That business last year with Sean Flaherty and the Banks murder. I got a lot of gold stars for that one. Even got a private chat in his office."

"Impressive."

"He said he'd like to see me take the lieutenant's exam."

"Doubly impressive," I say. "So?"

"I told him thanks but it's not for me. Sittin' at a desk, it'd drive me nuts. I'm a street guy, always have been. What do I know about shuffling around papers in triplicate?"

"What did he say?"

Kleinschmidt smiles. "He got it. He said he shuffled a lot of papers when he came back from the war. Hated every minute of it. He's a cop's cop, if you know what I mean."

"I do."

"So what's the story, Joe?" Kleinschmidt asks.

"You were on the other side of the glass. You heard it."

"Makes no sense to me," he says.

"No, Sarge, I'll tell you what makes no sense. When I left her at the door, she was standing up and when I left she locked the door. A few minutes later, after the old guy jimmied the lock, we found her lying on the living room floor dead and if you can figure out how it happened you're a better man than I am."

"The corner of the coffee table. She tripped."

"Over what? Her shadow? She was alone in that bungalow when I left it. Alone and alive."

"You say."

"We've been down this road before, Sarge. You really think I killed the woman?"

"Probably not," he concedes grudgingly.

"Then tell him to let me go."

"I can tell him but it's his case. His call. Come on, Joe, think about it. First you break into her bungalow using a set of lock picks. You hide under her bed. Then she cuts you with some shears and you hit her in the eye. You say you leave her alive. You're gone what? Ten or twelve minutes. You come back and find her dead on the floor. The door had been locked and all the windows were either locked from the inside or painted shut. Califano's slow and steady but he's not stupid. He thinks he has you cold. My advice? Call Ray Giordano."

I glance at my watch. "It's past midnight."

"Call him. You're going to need him."

He's right. When Califano returns, he arrests me on suspicion of murder. I find out later he had run everything past the watch commander who told him to push the button. I find out also that Califano gave the whole damned story to Lou Cioffi, the crime beat reporter for the L.A. Times. Great. Notoriety in tomorrow's edition. Just what I need.

At one o'clock I get to make my one phone call and I call Ray. He's not only a good friend, he's one of the few decent lawyers I know. We play basketball on Saturdays at the local Y and at times we are tight as brothers. He's not happy about the hour but he gets out of bed, dresses and shows up at division headquarters just before two a.m. They put us into a little room where we can talk in private. He is reassuring. He is positive he can get me out of here on OR within the hour. OR stands for "Own Recognizance".

I tell him my story from beginning to end, omitting nothing. He listens intently. At first he takes notes. Then he stops. Then he puts his notepad and pencil back in his pocket. When I finish he looks at me dolefully and tells me that OR probably isn't going to happen. He's going to need to see the police report first thing in the morning. He'll also talk to one of the assistant D.A.s who might cut me some temporary slack and if there's an autopsy he'll review that as well. He tells me not to worry. He's dealt with tougher cases than this one. He says it like he's a Christian about to go up against a hungry lion. Before he goes I ask one last favor. I don't know what the telephone situation is so I ask him to call Barry Loeb at the Morris office and tell him the ownership rights to my novel have been cleared up and he can start negotiating with RKO.

County jail isn't a lot of fun. It's past three o'clock when they finally finish with the mug shot and the fingerprints and they book me in for the night. I'm sharing a cell with a guy whose name I don't get because he's dead asleep and doesn't awaken even though I am making enough noise to send the cockroaches scurrying for cover. There's no shortage of yelling and crying and snoring and I doubt I will be getting much sleep. It's the only thing I get right all night. I don't doze off, not even for a second.

At seven o'clock I get breakfast. Tasteless hot cereal, apple juice and hot coffee. We march back to our cells by seven-thirty. My cell mate is awake now but I still don't know his name because he seems reluctant to give it. Maybe five-seven at best and probaby weighing in at around 250 pounds, he is singularly uncommunicative. Perhaps conversation violates his religion. And, oh, yes, he smells like a stable.

One of the jailers who is so good looking I suspect him of being a would-be actor, slips me a copy of the early edition of the L.A. Times. Maybe he thinks I can do him some good when I get out of Folsom thirty years from now. "Page 9" he whispers as he hands me the paper.

On my bunk, I lay back and turn to page 9. There it is and there is nothing to like about it. POETESS FOUND DEAD, it blares and below that, the subhead, WARNER BROTHERS EXEC HELD. The by-line is Lou Cioffi who is the Times' crime beat reporter. It isn't lengthy because there isn't a lot to write about but Cioffi gets my name spelled right. A "highly placed source close to the investigation" (read Califano) has described the killing as 'mysterious' and 'bizarre' but doesn't go into a lot of detail. Blow to the victim's face. Bloody head wound. When asked about motive, the "source" has no comment. Witnesses? We are talking to neighbors. Confession? Not yet.

I try to picture what's happening at the studio. Doubtless Jack Warner is livid. He likes publicity but not this kind. Charlie Berger is probably trying to cover for me. Glenda Mae is fending off phone calls. My three Oscar ladies, if they have read the story, are doubtless contemplating other avenues of publicity and I could hardly blame them. I wonder if the story has hit the New York papers and if Bunny knows what's happening. I have this urge to hear her voice.

A figure looms up over me. It's my cellmate without a name.

"Gimmee your change," it says.

He outweighs me by a hundred pounds and his hands are like

Virginia hams. I dig in my pocket and give him what I've got. He takes it without a word. I figure he needs it for a phone call but, no, he gets back onto his bunk, curls up and goes back to sleep. No problem. Whatever he wants is fine with me.

Ray shows up just before ten, exuding his usual aura of optimism.

"So far the case against you is relatively weak," he says.

Not VERY weak. RELATIVELY weak. I don't know what that means.

"Mostly circumstantial," he says.

I point out that the circumstances don't look good.

"They could be worse," he says. "For one thing, they can't come up with a decent motive other than this silly plagiarism thing." He laughs. "Good thing you didn't publicly threaten her."

Wait til they talk to Chaz Lambo at RKO who heard me say I was thinking of throttling the thief with my bare hands.

"Have they found anyone who saw me leave the bungalow with Virginia standing alive in the doorway?" I ask.

"Not yet," Ray says.

"Well, all those units, it takes a lot of time to cover them all."

"Actually," Ray says, "they're pretty much finished. Look, Joe," he continues hesitantly, "there are such things as diminished capacity, temporary insanity, accidental death."

I look at him hard. "I didn't kill her."

"Of course you didn't," he smiles, not believing a word of it. I figure by now he has looked at Califano's police report. I'm pretty sure I know what it says. If I were him, I wouldn't believe me either.

"Any luck with the D.A.'s office?" I ask.

He shakes his head.

"Look, Ray, forget the police report. Forget the D.A. Forget everything. You know me and you know I would never harm another human being. So, yeah, it looks bad but there is an explanation and I am not part of it. This you have got to believe."

He looks into my eyes and then he nods. "Of course. You're absolutely right. I just let the facts of the case confuse me." He shakes his head slowly. "A locked door, sealed windows, the victim left alive and alone and fifteen minutes later she's dead on the floor. Wow."

I nod in agreement. Wow.

Ray goes off to solve the insoluble.

He doesn't but six hours later someone else does.

The jailer comes by at three o'clock and leads me to a small room where Ray and Sergeant Califano are waiting for me.

Ray strides toward me, hand out, and grinning. "You were right. There was another explanation. We just got the coroner's report. The bloody bump on the head? Superficial. Cause of death? Poison."

"Poison?" I can't believe it. And then I'm thinking back to those few moments before I left the bungalow, when Virginia grimaced in pain, thinking it was an attack by her peptic ulcer.

"Cyanide. You're off the hook, Joe," Ray says.

"Not so fast on that, counselor," Califano says.

"Come on, Sergeant, without the blow to the head, you've got nothing."

"Not yet," Califano says, moving toward the door. "Get your stuff and get out of here," he says to me, "but don't leave the city. I don't want to have to chase after you." He goes out.

"He's pissed," I say.

"You read the story in the Times? Now he looks like a jerk," Ray says. "He'll do everything he can to make a case against you."

"Lucky me," I say. I've been debating whether I should reveal the spasm of pain Virginia endured but given Califano's frame of mind, I think I'd better wait and see how things play out.

We go out into the booking area so I can retrieve my personal belongings. Califano is there talking to a woman and a man. There's something about her that seems familiar. She glances in my direction and her expression hardens. She starts toward me with fire in her eyes.

"You son of a bitch!" she screams. "You killed my sister!"

Instinctively I back up as Ray tries to cut her off. Califano and the guy hurry after her. Ray has her by the wrist when the guy wraps his arms around her waist and pulls her away. "Livvy, no!" he says.

"Let me go, Alex!" she says angrily, continuing to struggle. "This bastard killed Ginny."

"No, maybe not," the man called Alex says. "Now calm down."

Califano head nods to a nearby cop who comes over and takes hold of the woman who has started to cry miserably. The cop and Califano lead her away. The guy stays. I have figured out that the familiar looking woman is Virginia's sister Olivia and the guy is Olivia's slick boyfriend.

"Alex Farnsworth," he says offering his hand. I take it. We shake. When I get my hand back I do not count my fingers despite Maybelle Ruskin's description of him. Ray introduces himself. They also shake.

"I apologize for Olivia, Mr. Bernardi," he says. "She is terribly distraught. As sisters they were very close. This is a terrible blow."

I think back to my conversation with Maybelle. This filial devotion is not what I had been led to believe.

"For me as well, Mr, Farnsworth. I did not know Virginia well but I had reason to like and admire her."

"As we all did. I guess it was all too much for her," he says.

That's an odd remark, I think. "What do you mean?"

He shrugs. "I think it's obvious. Maybelle Ruskin filled us in about Ginny's theft of your book. For someone as vulnerable as Ginny I'm sure the thought of public scorn and humiliation was more than she was ready to bear."

"Suicide?"

"Unless you poisoned her, Mr. Bernardi, which I seriously doubt, I don't see any other explanation."

I shake my head. "No. She was embarrassed and contrite but not suicidal. I'd bet my life on it."

He smiles ironically. "Given the circumstances, you may be doing just that. Anyway, we didn't come here to give you a hard time. We're here to see about claimng the body for burial."

"Of course."

"Mother Jenks is a devout Christian," Farnsworth says, "and all she can think about now is the funeral service. It is quite a problem getting her anywhere and it takes monumental planning." Off my look, he continues. "I'm sorry, did I not mention that the girls' mother is bedridden and has been so for several years now?"

"No, I'm sorry to hear it," I say.

"Multiple strokes right after the war ended. They left her unable to walk. Luckily her late husband left her extremely well off but even so to get her to the church and the cemetery will require a special ambulance, a motorized wheelchair, breathing apparatus, a nurse and a doctor standing by at all times. All this has put Olivia into a frenzy and she is not acting herself."

"That's a lot of pressure," I say.

"Indeed."

"I'd also say that whatever Mother wanted or demanded, she got without question."

He nods. "Without question."

"Well, please convey to Olivia and to her mother my deep sympathy on their loss. I can assure you I had nothing whatever to do with Virginia's death. You think it may be suicide. I don't, and if possible, I'll do what I can to find out who is actually responsible."

Farnsworth nods with a smile. "Thank you, Mr. Bernardi. I'm sure they will both appreciate your sentiments. And now if you will excuse me, I had better get back to Livvy."

He walks off. Ray watches him go, then turns to me.

"Smooth," he says.

"Like thirty-year-old scotch," I say.

CHAPTER TEN

I go back to the office for want of anything better to do. It's well past five o'clock but Glenda Mae is still there like Horatio at the bridge. Despite her soft and southern gentility she's a pretty tough cookie and she's been guarding my honor, my reputation and my privacy with exceptional fortitude but when I walk through the door, she almost bursts into tears. She leaps up from her chair and throws her arms around me and holds me close.

"Whoa!" I say. "What will Beau say?" Beau's her husband. He's an auto mechanic and probably makes more money than I do.

"Screw Beau," she says, looking me in the eye. "Are you okay?"

"I'm fine," I say.

She cranes for a close look at the bandage on my neck. "That doesn't look fine," she says.

"An accident. It was all a big mixup."

"Some mixup when they toss you in jail," she says disbelievingly. She's waiting for an explanation.

I shrug. "Okay, okay. I broke into her bungalow at the Garden of Allah to try to find the typewriter that was used to re-type my novel because I was pretty sure it wasn't her but her old boyfriend who died a couple of months ago who could have been poisoned but probably not but the problem was, she caught me hiding under the bed. Well, I wasn't exactly under the bed when she caught me but she did have a pair of shears in her hand and we started to wrestle, just a little and---"

She puts up her hand. "All right, that's enough. I'll wait for the movie," she says.

"I thought you might," I reply. "So who wants me?

"Everybody but you'd better start with Mr. Berger."

I nod. He would have been my first guess.

I start out.

"By the way, there's a casserole in your desk," she says.

"What?"

"Compliments of Bert and Eleanor. They wanted you to know how good those recipes really are."

"What kind is it?"

"Eggplant."

"I hate eggplant."

"I know," she says. "Beau loves eggplant."

I can only shake my head. "Take it."

"Thanks, boss," she says.

"And go home."

"Yes, boss."

She smiles and heads for my private office in search of eggplant.

Charlie is seated at his desk, eyes closed as if he is in deep thought. When I rap on the door jamb, his eyes pop open and his head snaps up. At 61 Charlie is prone to catnaps though he will claim otherwise. He has a penchant for merely 'resting his eyes'.

"Looking for me?" I say cheerily as I walk in.

"Not really," Charlie says. "I knew where you were all day long if I needed you. What have you stepped in now, Joe?"

"Do you really want to know?" I ask.

"Not really but J.L. may want to know and I don't wish to appear a dunce."

I sit and recount the entire story from Barry's revelation of theft to my grudging release earlier this afternoon. Charlie listens intently. He does not take notes. Even as I am talking he is figuring a way to pass this information on to Mr. Warner in the best light possible. When I'm finished he just shakes his head.

"Joe, how do you get yourself into these things?"

"Well, it ain't easy," I say, mimicking a line from Mortimer Snerd, Edgar Bergen's dimwitted dummy.

"Our job is to manipulate the news, shape the news, and spread the news. Not BE the news."

"Right," I say.

"Well, I suppose on the positive side you've been released. Does this mean you've been cleared?"

"Not exactly."

"Oh, Christ," he mutters under his breath. "I may have to suspend you until this gets straightened out."

"Please do," I say. "Eleanor Parker's sending me casseroles."

"No," he says in disbelief.

"Jawohl," I say.

"We'll forget suspension," he says.

"I thought we might," I say.

"But I want you steering clear of these people and the police. You come to work, you keep your head down, you do your job. That's it. Understand?"

"I'll do my best," I say.

"You'll do it," Charlie says testily.

I shake my head. "Charlie, I may still be suspect numero uno."

"Or they may rule it a suicide."

"They won't and it wasn't. That's not how I left her."

Charlie shakes his head. "Joe, you're putting me in a tough position."

"Mine's tougher, Charlie," I tell him. "Until the cops come up with a better suspect than me. I'm not going to sit around like a target at a turkey shoot waiting for the bullet with my name on it. Besides I won't be much good to you sitting in a jail cell."

He leans forward, jabbing a finger in my direction. "You end up in a jail cell again and Warner Brothers will claim they never heard of you."

"Ohmigod," I gasp. "Back to Continental Studios?"

"If you're lucky," Charlie says.

I promise Charlie that I will behave myself, causing only small ripples, not waves, and that the studio's well being will always be paramount in my mind. When I see that Charlie has bought this load of malarkey, I take my leave. I don't want to go home but I realize I have to be somewhere so I head for the house. I pick up dinner on the way, a six-pack and a bag of chips. I plan to eat the chips, down all six cans of beer and hope that the effect will be to put me to sleep so I can catch up on what I lost last night in jail.

I'm on beer three when the phone rings. Because it might be Bunny, I answer it.

"Joe, it's Barry," he says.

"Hi," I say.

"Did I catch you at a bad time?" he asks.

"Just getting a little sloshed. What's up?"

"I just got out of a two hour marathon with RKO."

"And?"

"They're not interested."

"What?" I am stunned.

"Not in V.J. Shelley and not in you. The material, they said, is in question."

"No, no, Barry. Their brains are in question. Their taste is in question."

"Yeah, we know that, Joe, but Chaz Lambo is a certifiable coward without the courage of his convictions if he had any which he doesn't. According to him, the provenance is clouded."

"He said that?" I ask.

"He did," Barry says.

"Who wrote it down for him?"

"The moron on the next rung up the ladder," Barry says.

"Barry, the woman admitted to everything."

"The girl's dead, Joe."

"The typewriter is proof."

"Nobody's going to give a rat's ass about the typewriter. The girl spouting tears in front of a newsreel camera, that might have done it but we know that ain't gonna happen."

"Damn," I mutter under my breath.

"Look, Joe, don't sweat it. I checked your contract and I had it right. Warners gets first look at everything. RKO's in play only if Warners passes."

"Okay," I say, "how do we handle Warners?"

"The best way is to get it directly to a producer. Aren't you in tight with Henry Blanke?"

"Sure. Among others."

"Pick one."

"Let me think about it," I say. "What about Doubleday?"

Silence.

"Barry, are you there?"

More silence. Then:

"Pasadena." This is movie-guy talk for 'take your crummy work and shove it'.

"Why?"

"Same excuse. Whoever did this to you, the guy or the girl-friend, they screwed you royally, Joe. No publisher will touch it and that means the studios are out as well. You know how this town works. There are ninety-nine reasons out of a hundred to say no. Yours is a no-brainer. Your only chance is Warners."

"I'll get back to you," I say glumly.

"Make it quick," Barry says. "No matter how much they love you over there, guys like Henry can smell a dead fish from a mile away."

I hang up and make short work of the rest of beer number three. I fumble around for the church key and pop open number four. I am slightly loaded but not so loaded that I don't have a clear vision of the extent to which someone has screwed me. A few days ago I was ready to throttle V.J. Shelley. Now I want to execute whoever poisoned her and not only stole a young and vibrant life but also turned six years of my life into so much scrap paper. I vow to myself that this will not stand. I drain number four and start on number five.

I am sprawled on the sofa, beer in hand, feet up on the cof-fee table when I see the glint of a headlight at curbside in front of the house. I hope they are lost because I am in no mood for company. I'm having too much fun girding my loins for the com-bat to come. I look again and the car is still there. No question about it. I have company.

I go to the front door and open it just as Bunny hurries up the walkway toward the house. She squeals with dellght when she sees me and runs into my arms. I am stunned but still manage a big hug and an even bigger kiss which she returns with wild abandon.

"What are you doing here? You've got two more days in New York," I say.

"Ginger called me first thing this morning and read me the piece in the Times. I caught the first plane out. Are you okay?"

"Yeah, I'm fine, I think. Better now that you're here." I kiss her again. More response. This playful welcome is turning into something a lot more serious.

The cab driver is struggling up the walk with Bunny's suitcases. I tell him to put them just inside the front door. He says the meter's $9.70. I give him twelve bucks. I don't normally overtip like that but having Bunny home has fogged my brain. When the cabbie has left and the door is shut, I make another move on Bunny but now she's not playing. She's finally noticed the bandage on my neck. She wants to know what happened and she doesn't want the abridged edition. I tell it all to her finishing with the imminent demise of my novel. This really gets her because she loves the book even more than I do. She holds me close and I am being overcome by the smell of her and the soft warmth of her body.

"How was your trip?" I ask, as if at this moment I really care.

I feel her body tense for just a moment. "Later," she says, pulling me onto the sofa. She brushes away the empty chip bag and two empty beer cans and climbs on top of me. She grabs at my tie and yanks it off. Her eyes half close and her tongue is moistening her lips and all I can think of is, did I really have to drink those five beers tonight?

CHAPTER ELEVEN

It's daybreak. The cock would be crowing if we had a cock. Somehow during the night Bunny and I negotiated our way from the living room sofa into the bedroom and now we are all tangled up in the sheets. I make a move to get out of bed but Bunny yanks me by the ankle and brings me back. Tickle and tussle is her favorite game and we play it for a while until we come to grips with reality. I get the bathroom first because I will be done with it inside of ten minutes. I will then dress, grab a quick bite and walk outside to my car for the short drive to the studio. At that moment, Bunny will still be in the bathroom.

It's quarter to nine and Glenda Mae is already on duty, womanning her desk. I tell her I need Ray Giordano. Try his house first, then office. While she's dialing I pour myself a cup of coffee and go to my desk. In a moment she gives me a double beep on the intercom and I pick up the phone.

"Ray?"

"Yo."

"Sorry about the hour. This is urgent."

"Always is," he says.

"Did you get a look at the coroner's report?"

"Nope."

"No?"

"By the time it came through, you'd been released. I no longer had a right to see it."

"Damn."

"One thing I did hear. Unofficial and off the record from a friend in the morgue."

"What?"

"She may have taken a suicide pill," Ray says.

"Bullshit."

"That's what I hear."

"What is this, some kind of war movie? I don't believe it."

"Up to you," Ray says.

"Thanks, old buddy."

"Happy to help."

I hang up and buzz Glenda Mae. It's past nine and probably too early but I ask her to call Mocambo's and make a reservation for two for tonight. At some point last night, in the throes of passion, I promised to take Bunny for an evening of dining and dancing to which she readily agreed, especially since her absolute favorite, Frankie Laine, is in town for a one-night stand. Then I ask her to get me Sergeant Kleinschmidt. Both his numbers, home and headquarters, are in my wheeldex. She buzzes me back in five minutes. Mocambo's isn't picking up. She'll try later. As for Kleinschmidt, no answer at home. She left word at headquarters.

I sip my coffee and lean back in my chair. After a decent night's sleep, I am confronted with many scenarios but suicide is not one of them. I am positive someone killed Virginia but I don't know who and I don't know how and I really don't know how to begin to find out.

The intercom buzzes. I flip it on. "Wyman", Glenda Mae says. Oh, boy, I think. Now what?

"Jane!" I greet her ebulliently.

"Joe, how are you? I was told the terrible news. Are you okay? Have they let you go? I'm sure it was all a terrible mixup."

I tell her I'm fine and there is nothing to worry about.

"I am so glad to hear that," she says. "I would hate to lose you."

"No chance of that." I say.

Satisfied that I am back at the helm, she launches into a lengthy account of her activities at her old high school in St. Joseph, Missouri. The screening of 'Johnny Belinda' was a rousing success. Tons of photos are on the way along with copies of the stories from the local papers. But the news is even better, she says, and here's the surprise. The following night was homecoming and the senior prom and when the faculty and students begged her to stay on, she had no choice.

"I danced the night away, Joe," she says excitedly. "The lindy hop, even a jitterbug. Took 'em all on. Half the football team, the class president, the homecoming king. I used to be a hoofer, you know. And you cannot believe the pictures we have. Anyway, everything should be on your desk in a couple of days."

"Can't wait," I say.

On to Florida, she tells me, and hangs up. I have this sudden picture of her going alligator hunting in the Everglades with a cameraman right on her tail. Surely she is not that reckless. Then I remember that there is an Oscar at stake. Que sera sera.

Heeding Charlie Berger's admonition, I decide to settle into some work. I ask Glenda Mae to order up several hundred glossies of Tennessee Williams and then I slip a sheet of paper into my typewriter and start to write:

EXCLUSIVE TO YOU IN YOUR AREA
TENNESSEE WILLIAMS THRILLED TO BE PART OF
MENAGERIE FILMING

*"I'm really looking forward to the next few months,"
Tennessee Williams said as Warner Brothers prepares to film the
movie version of his hit Broadway play, 'The Glass Menagerie'.
"I couldn't be more delighted about the cast that producer Jerry
Wald and director Irving Rapper has assembled. Jane Wyman
will be brilliant as Laura and I see another Oscar in her future.
And Gertrude Lawrence as Amanda. What a coup. A great lady
of the stage taking on a part that she was made for...."*

It goes on like that for another 250 words, me quoting
Williams with words he never said. But that, alas, is the job.
Anything and everything to get the fannies in theater seats all
over the country. That's how the game is played. After lunch I
will be concocting a similar release featuring Gertrude Lawrence
lavishing praise on everyone in sight but particularly Tennessee
Williams. I distinctly remember her describing the screenplay as
'so well written, so well defined'. This press release may actually
have a ring of truth to it.

When I get back from lunch I find a note that Eleanor Parker's
husband, Bert, has called. I return it immediately. For starters he
wants to know how the casserole was. I tell him it couldn't have
been more appreciated. He is greatly pleased. He says he has
hit on a great idea for national coverage. Eleanor and a camera crew will go into a woman's prison and in a twenty-minute
two-reeler expose the terrible conditions that exist. I point out
to Bert that, given the subject matter, no warden with even half
a brain will let Eleanor within a mile of the prison gates. There
is silence. How about if Eleanor and a camera crew go into the
prison and film a deeply caring medical staff working hard to
rehabilitate the prisoners in advance of their release back into
society? I tell him that approach has a much better chance of
getting made though I'm not sure how much exposure I can get

for it. Bert's not worried. Just put the babes in short skirts and low cut tops. I tell him I'll give it a lot of thought and at the first opportunity, I hang up.

I buzz Glenda Mae. I tell her if any calls from the island of Aruba come through to say that I am out of the office and not expected for several days.

At that moment the phone rings. It's Sergeant Kleinschmidt returning my call.

"What's up?" he says.

"I need a favor."

"Shoot."

"I need to look at the autopsy report."

"What for?"

"A lot of people are talking suicide. I don't believe it."

"Coulda happened," he says.

"Unless she was being interrogated by the Gestapo, I don't think so."

"Her body was laced with cyanide," Kleinschmidt says. "She presented all the classical symptoms of the poison, reddening of the skin, the faint smell of bitter almonds---"

"You've seen the report----"

"And the medical examiner found a partially digested gelatin capsule in her stomach."

"That changes things," I say.

"Yes, it does. The coroner's calling it suicide, Joe, and Califano's going along with it. The good news is you're off the hook."

"Yeah. Good news," I say and even as I say it, I still don't believe it. The woman I left in that doorway was not suicidal. Not even close.

For quite a long time I sit at my desk, yellow lined pad in my lap, doodling aimlessly. I do this a lot when looking for inspiration. Sometimes it works. Mostly I just waste yellow lined paper. Then I get an idea. It isn't much of one. Kind of a goofy long shot but it's better than wearing out the seat of my pants in the office. I head out.

As I pass by Glenda Mae's desk and tell her I'll be gone for the rest of the day, I notice a box on her desk.

"What's that?" I ask.

"Pie," she says.

"Where did it come from?" I ask.

"Where do you think?" she says. "Warner Brothers very own Betty Crocker."

"What kind?"

"Rutabaga."

"I hate rutabaga."

"I know."

"Let me guess. Beau loves rutabaga."

"Adores it," she says.

"Take it," I say.

"Thanks, boss."

At the door, I turn. "If a chocolate cake shows up, tell Beau he's out of luck."

"I think he knows that," she says.

"Have a nice evening."

"Same to you."

It takes me twenty-five minutes to get to the Garden of Allah. I pull into the parking area and come to a stop. As I get out of my car and look around my impressions from the other day are confirmed. The asphalt in the parking area is cracking as are the walkways. The lawn is getting minimal care at best. The main building is in bad need of a paint job. I see scraps of paper and empty beer and soda cans in a couple of the flower beds. The once proud landmark is losing its beauty like Margo in 'Lost Horizon'. Although I have no vested interest, I feel sad about it. The ever changing face of Hollywood, not always for the better.

I go in search of Oswald Pennybaker. Instinct tells me that if he had been close to Virginia, their units should be near to one another so I turn down the same path I took the other day. Sure enough, I see him down near the end. He's on his knees, tending to his flower beds. He looks up at me as I draw near.

"I see they let you go, young fella," he says.

"They did, Mr. Pennybaker. Not much to hold me on as it turned out."

He nods. "Cyanide. Hard to figure."

I'm surprised by this. The old codger has to be wired in tight with somebody to know about the pill. I guess being a former police chief has its privileges.

He gets to his feet, spryly for a man his age. "Guess you came down to chat," he says.

"Among other things," I say.

"Can I offer you a cold beer?" he asks.

"You can," I say.

"Set on the stoop," he says. "I'd ask you in but the place is a mess." He starts for the door. "Be right out."

I sit and in a moment he's back out with a couple of tall cold bottles. He's already uncapped them. I take one and drink deep. It tastes good. He does likewise.

"Guess you've been around here quite a while," I venture.

"Twenty years, give or take a couple of months. Came here in '29 with my granddaughter. She'd done some acting locally in Ukiah, had it in her mind she'd like to get into the movies. Her folks wouldn't hear of it until I volunteered to take her. Had nothing better to do. Tired of chasing bad guys."

"How'd it work out?" I ask.

"Well enough for the first two or three years," he says. "Lily had a good speaking voice-- that was her name, Lily--- and the talkies were just coming in. She got a lot of small parts. Made a good living. That and my pension, we did okay."

"But nothing lasts forever."

He looks at me with a wry smile. "You got that right, son." He takes a long pull on his beer and I think he's through. But he continues. "She met a fella. Pretty worthless but she went for him. I warned her but she wasn't listening. She started staying out late, then not coming home. Next thing you know she's carrying this fella's baby. He finds out and he doesn't come around anymore. Liked to kill her. She says, it's okay, Grandpa. It's our baby. We'll raise him up. He'll be okay, you'll see. That was Lily, always seeing the good side of everything. And then one day she got these cramps and I got her to the hospital and she had some kind of poisoning on account of the baby and then the baby aborted. Stillborn. And the next day, Lily died."

I can only shake my head. "I am so sorry," I say. It isn't much.

"The fella's name was Donaldson. Ray. Roy. Something like that. I caught up with him at a bar in West Hollywood. I put a gun in his back and drove him out to the Mojave desert on the way to Barstow. We turned off the main road about a half mile to this dry creek bed. I made him get out of the car and then I put a bullet in his head. Coulda buried him, I suppose, but thought maybe it was more fitting if I left him for the coyotes. I was able to get back home in time for supper."

I don't know what you're supposed to say when someone tells you something like that so I don't say anything.

"Coulda gone back to Ukiah, I suppose," Oswald continues, "but I just didn't feel like it, so I stayed on. Worked at security now and then. Some private investigating. Not much and not often but I got by."

"Then Virginia moved in," I say.

He looks over at me with a half smile on his face.

"That's right," he says.

"And she reminded you a lot of Lily."

"That's right, too. Not that they looked alike. It was just something about the way they carried themselves, the way they looked at you and the way they laughed when something tickled them."

I nod. "Losing Virginia. You've been hit hard."

"Hard enough," he says. He takes another long pull in his beer and stares across the walkway to her unit, two doors down. "Whatever it is, son, get to it."

"Excuse me?" I say lamely.

He looks at me intently and now I see the flint in his gray-blue eyes. "You didn't come all the way over here just to chat. Whatever's eatin' at you, get to it."

I meet his gaze and I am in silent awe. 83 years old and he has lost none of his instincts. There is no question. He is the same cop who was terrorizing Ukiah's criminal element thirty years ago.

"It's my guess Virginia was pretty much a loner," I say.

"She was."

"Who were her friends? Who came to see her in her home?"

"Aside from me?"

"Aside from you."

"Her agent, Maybelle Ruskin."

"I know her," I say. "That's one."

"Charlotte Schroeder."

"Older woman? Wears funny hats?"

"That's her. Leon's mother. Came by a lot when he was alive. Still comes by now and then. She and Virginia seemed to be close."

"Anyone else?"

"Her sister Olivia showed up one day uninvited. Virginia wouldn't let her in. Never did find out how she got the address."

"Is that it?"

"That's it," he says. "What's your point?"

"I don't believe that Virginia killed herself."

He nods. "We agree on that."

"I believe she was murdered and I think I know how," I say.

"I'm listening," he says.

I tell him my theory. When I finish, he nods. "Coulda happened that way."

"We need to prove it," I say.

"Her bungalow's a crime scene. Be breaking the law to let ourselves in," he says..

"It would," I say.

"A year in jail. Maybe more."

"Wouldn't doubt it."

"You still got that set of lock picks?" he asks.

"I do," I say.

"Then lets mosey over," he says, getting to his feet.

No one's watching and even if they were, I don't care. We walk up the front door. In a matter of a few seconds I've jimmied the lock and we're inside. We head straight for the bathroom where I open the medicine cabinet door. It's filled with medicinal aids like aspirin and bandages, cold creams, mascara, eye liner and a prescription bottle from a local pharmacy. I hand it to Oswald to open. Inside are a couple of dozen gelatin capsules. Doubtless this is the medicine prescribed to deal with Virginia's peptic ulcer. Oswald takes out two capsules and hands me one. I twist it and it comes apart easily, its contents spilling into the sink. Oswald and I share a look. I am positive my theory has been confirmed.

Within the past few days or maybe the past few weeks, someone has entered this bungalow, either by invitation or by breaking in, and has substituted a capsule laced with cyanide for the ingredients of her prescription. It is a near perfect method of killing. At some time in the future--- a day, a week, a month-- Virginia will take the fatal pill and the killer will be elsewhere. Virginia is reclusive and lives alone, the poison works almost immediately. It can hardly fail.

I think about the sleazy coward who has done this and I literally want to vomit. Most of the time I'm a guy who loves life but there are other times when I feel the world is one gigantic cesspool. This is one of those times.

CHAPTER TWELVE

swald and I walk to the parking lot. The next step is simple. Oswald calls Sergeant Califano. He'll apologize for not telling the sergeant about Virginia's ulcer medicine. He's heard about the so-called suicide attempt but can't believe it. It's far more likely that she swallowed a prescription capsule to treat her ulcer and it is perhaps not likely but still possible that the capsules were tampered with. If Califano could check out Virginia's medicine chest, forensics might be able to tell if the half digested capsule in her system matches the ones in her prescription bottle.

Oswald and I are pretty sure the police lab will find they're identical and the coroner's report will be amended to specify murder as the cause of death. Cyanide poisoning is an ugly way to die and Virginia didn't deserve it. One way or another Oswald and I are determined to ferret out whoever was responsible.

I head for home with a heavy heart and a lot on my mind and it must have been pretty obvious because when I walk in the door, Bunny takes one look at me and says "What?" It's not a question, it's a wide-eyed interjection.

"What what?" I say, avoiding reality. She is dressed to kill in lavender satin and cultured pearls, guaranteed to overwhelm

Frankie Laine should he look in her direction. I trot out my most innocent smile. Nothing's wrong. There are no problems.

Bunny is not that easily fooled.

"What happened?" she asks.

"Nothing. Everything's fine."

"Joe," she says, 'there is a reason why you always lose at poker and I'm at looking at it. What's going on?"

"I think I need a beer," I say heading for the kitchen. I take out a cold one and open it as Bunny follows me into the kitchen. She stares at me, arms folded across her chest, waiting.

I'm caught and I know it so I sit down and lay it all out. As she listens she,too, sits. I can see it in her eyes. She's feeling Virginia's pain as well as mine. When I'm finished she shakes her head sadly.

"Not a good night for kicking up our heels," she says,

"No, it's not," I agree.

"How about chow mein at Henry Ling's?" she suggests.

"Terrific," I say. "But Frankie's going to miss you."

"He'll get over it," she says as she gets up and goes in to change into something more fitting for a neighborhood greasy spoon.

I drink a little more beer and contemplate what a lucky guy I am to have found a dame like Bunny. Not even the good days with my ex-wife Lydia were as good as these. I think maybe the time has come to try the marriage scene again. I'm pretty sure I'm ready. I'm not so sure about Bunny. She's always avoided any serious talk about it. Maybe she's changed, too. Maybe tonight I'll broach the subject once again.

The phone rings. The kitchen unit's on the wall behind me. I answer it.

"Hello."

"Hi. Joe? It's Walt."

"Walt?"

"Walt Davenport. Colliers."

"Oh, sure. Hi."

You could chip ice off of every syllable.

"Did I catch you at a bad time? I need to speak to Bunny," he says.

"Actually, Walt, we're headed out to dinner and we're already late for our reservation." As if Henry Ling even knew what a reservation was.

"Oh, too bad." The disappointment in his voice sounds genuine. "Well, it'll keep. Tell her I'll call tomorrow at her office." Guess he must think I'm her private secretary.

"I'll tell her," I say.

"Great. Thanks. Toodle-oo." And he hangs up.

What kind of a man says 'toodle-oo', I ask myself. Eastern people are funny.

A few minutes later, as we're headed out the door, Bunny asks, "While I was in the bathroom, did I hear the phone ring?"

"It was your friend Walt from New York," I say. "He said he'd call you at the office tomorrow."

To this, she nods and gets in the passenger seat. She has no comment about the guy I caught in her hotel room at two in the morning ostensibly working as if there weren't twenty-three other hours in the day. But I let it go.

Henry is glad to see us. Henry is actually glad to see anyone as his emporium has never experienced landslide business. The food is wildly unpredictable. We know. We've tried most of it. But the chow mein and the chicken fried rice and the won ton soup are always excellent so we settle for our usual fare. We chat quietly about this and that throughout the meal but when it comes time for the green tea ice cream, I can't take any more.

"So," I say, "your pal Walt. Tell me about him."

She looks up sharply and I've caught her by surprise. She's the second worst poker player at the table. "There's nothing to tell," she says.

"Really? Is he short, tall, fat, balding, married, divorced, looking?" I put special emphasis on that last word.

She scowls at me. "Oh, for God's sakes, Joe."

"Just asking," I say innocently.

"He's the editor in chief of a major national magazine and he's taken a shine to me."

"I'll bet," I say.

"He thinks I have talent," she replies a little testily.

"Okay," I say.

"From a man like him, that is a huge compliment."

"Okay," I repeat. I stare into her eyes. I'm an excellent starer. She turns her attention to her ice cream. When she looks back up, I'm still staring.

'What?" she says.

"You tell me."

After a moment she puts her spoon down.

"He's offered me a job," she says, finally.

I think my eyes widen, just like in a bad movie.

"What?"

She shakes her head. "Don't worry. I turned him down."

"A job doing what?"

"Associate editor. It's not the top but it's nowhere near the bottom. I told him I was very flattered but it wasn't possible."

"Do you think he heard you?" I ask.

"Of course."

"Then why's he calling?"

"Because he's persistent." I think I already knew that. "Joe, I said no. I meant no. I'm not going anywhere."

I look into her eyes, trying to read her. I know what she said. Now I'm trying to figure what she meant. I take a bite of ice cream.

"Did you give it any thought?" I ask.

"No. Yes. No." She sighs. "I'm not interested."

"Maybe you should be," I say.

"What's that supposed to mean?"

"It means you're a very talented young woman who has made a name for herself here in Los Angeles and now has a chance to succeed on the national scene and you can't just dismiss it out of hand."

"It would mean moving to New York. I won't do that."

"What have you got against New York?" I ask.

"You," she says.

I reach across the table and take her hand and squeeze it. I'd been in the verge of proposing marriage. Now I know I can't. It would be seen as a weapon to tie her to me unfairly. Every ounce of my body screams out for her to stay but I don't want her to sacrifice any sort of dream she might have for me, as much as we might love one another. Whether she likes it or not she has to give this some serious consideration and think with her head and not just her heart.

"Sleep on it, Bunny," I say. "Tonight, tomorrow, the next night. Talk to this man. Weigh everything. Then when you're sure, we'll talk."

She looks at me a little fearfully. "Do you want me to take it?"

I shake my head. "No. But I want you to either take it or refuse it for the right reasons and I want you to be sure. The love that you and I have for one another is immense but in the end it may not be enough. Be sure, Bunny. I don't want you waking up someday hating me."

She looks away. The process has begun.

The next day I am very busy. The Louisiana Association of Entertainment Editors is in town and Charlie has fobbed them off on me. Including lunch, a tour of the facilities and a visit to stage 8 where John Garfield and Pat Neal are filming a scene for 'The Breaking Point', my day is pretty much shot so I use the time between nine and ten to good advantage. I call Oswald Pennybaker and he says he has talked to Califano. The sergeant was none too happy but promised to look into the pill situation, Then I call Phineas Ogilvy at the Times to ask a favor. Over the years he has owed me a bushel of them and he never reneges. I tell him about the developments surrounding Virginia Jenks' death, i.e. my certainty that it was murder and how it was done and the fact that the cops are reopening the case. I'm jumping the gun a little here but I want to goad Califano into action and there's nothing like a newspaper story to get a cop's attention. There's also nothing like a cop's attention to get a killer feeling a lot less secure and that's the whole idea. Phineas will take all of this to Lou Cioffi, the crime beat reporter who nailed me with the first story and if we're lucky Lou's new story will roil the nest of snakes and hopefully get somebody to do something stupid.

At five-fifteen I am done with my charges from the Bayou State. They will be descending en masse at Ciro's that evening and Bunny's boss, Billy Wilkerson, who owns Ciro's as well as The Hollywood Reporter, will separate the revelers from their expense accounts quickly and quietly. They don't call it a tourist trap for nothing. I am too savvy to be caught dead in a place like that so tonight Bunny and I are going to sashay down to Mocambo's for an evening of dining and dancing and listening to Frankie Laine who has been held over an additional night. Having taken positive steps in my quest for justice I am no longer morose and Bunny is determined to wear that satin lavender outfit even if she has to wear it to the zoo. I have made up my mind that, no matter what, I will not query her about any phone call she might have gotten from amiable Walt from NYC and if it means getting drunk, so be it. Tonight, madcap fun will prevail.

Glenda Mae has gone for the weekend but before she left she's opened the Herald-Examiner to one of the back pages and circled something in red. I check it out. It's a notice of an art exhibit the following evening at a place called Le Chalet d'Arte on Rodeo Drive, curator Olivia Jenks. I chuckle to myself. Not only does this place not know whether it's French or Italian, it has a curator, just like your friendly neighborhood museum. The little notice warns us that the works of renowned neo-impressionist Lazslo D'Allesandro will be on display, they will be for sale and treat of treats, the artist himself will be on hand to meet and greet you. I can hardly wait. Tomorrow evening at seven p.m. I plan to be at the chalet with Bunny on my arm, nibbling bruschetta, and continuing to roil snakes.

CHAPTER THIRTEEN

When it comes to snaring the public's attention, Olivia Jenks has obviously been taking lessons from P.T. Barnum or Cecil B. DeMille or maybe both. As soon as we turn off of Santa Monica Boulevard onto Rodeo Drive, we can see where we are headed. It's several blocks away but the street is jammed with traffic trying to avoid the valet parkers who are handling the first wave of arrivals anxious to feast their eyes on the wild imaginings of Lazslo D'Allesandro. We slide easily into the line and after ten minutes or so, an agile young man (most likely a UCLA undergrad) has traded a ticket for my car and we enter the chalet, smiling at the greeter as we do so. He is wearing morning clothes and as far as I can tell, he is not armed. Maybe he should be with all those valuable paintings on display.

The chalet is on the smallish side, Beverly Hills rents being what they are, but it's cleverly laid out making maximum use of the available space. There are paintings on the wall, paintings on easels and even a couple hanging by wires from the ceiling. I look down. The floor space is not being used. To our left I see a staircase which leads to a second floor and, I presume, more of the same.

Bunny looks ravishing. On the theory that the Beverly Hills hotsy- totsy crowd is not the same as the knuckle-headed tourist trade that frequents Mocambo's, she is again wearing the lavender satin outfit, this time with an aquamarine necklace and matching earrings. I am wearing an old suit. We are no more than ten yards into the main room when we are accosted by a pretty young thing in a french maid's costume carrying a tray of pate canapes. Bunny takes one. I ask if there is any bruschetta. She just smiles. English may be a chore for her.

Bunny wanders over to a near wall to inspect a colorful painting which appears to be a man in a jock strop and a top hat holding a cat upside down by its tail. Meanwhile I am casting my gaze around the room trying to spot the curator, Olivia Jenks. In my jacket pocket I have a copy of Lou Cioffi's story that appeared in today's Times. Lou outdid himself. It is magnificently lurid, points fingers in every direction and gives the impression that the cops are only moments away from making an arrest. I couldn't have written it better myself.

"What do you think?" Bunny asks me, still eying the painting.

"I think the guy's overdressed," I say.

"I like the cat," she says. Bunny Lesher, art critic. "I think I'll wander for a bit," she says.

I nod. This is code for, I'm going to walk around and see how many handsome young men try to pick me up. Bunny has just turned 29 but she's already started to worry about age lines and sagging flesh. She needs reinforcement. If it makes her happy, I'm all for it.

I, too, wander and I am rewarded when I spot Olivia Jenks off in a corner standing next to a hulk of a man in an ill-fitting black suit and chatting effusively with Gloria deHaven and her husband John Payne. I sidle in their direction trying to get close enough to eavesdrop. I hear enough to learn that the hulk is the artist and that he should never wear black, not with his dandruff. Gloria has found a painting she adores. John isn't so sure though he does agree that it's a perfect size to cover the wall space that needs covering in their living room. I have heard that all is not well with the Paynes' marriage but it's not obvious here. Maybe the rumors are just that. Rumors.

Gloria and John amble off in search of another painting of the same dimensions and I seize the opportunity to intrude on Olivia and the guest of honor. She is momentarily polite because she thinks she recognizes me but when I introduce myself she freezes up like a Chevy crankshaft in a North Dakota blizzard. I, of course, ignore this and put out my hand to the hulk.

"Joe Bernardi," I say as we shake. Oddly he has a grip like Ethel Barrymore. "I'm flabbergasted to be here among all these indescribable paintings. They take my breath away."

"Dank you," he says. Dank as in wet and musty. As a cliche this guy is too good to be true. Where's he from? I'm betting on the Carpathian mountains.

"And you, Miss Jenks, you are looking lovely this evening."

"Thank you," she half smiles.

"And the turnout. Marvelous. The creme de la creme of Hollywood society. Your reputation in the art world is well deserved."

"You are most kind." Her eyes are scanning the crowd for a potential buyer because she's pretty sure I'm not here to buy even if I could afford it which she knows I can't.

"A pity all this has to take place under the terrible cloud of Virginia's murder," I say.

She looks at me sharply. "Murder?" Aha! She hasn't seen the article. I decide to enlighten her.

"Oh, yes. It was in the paper today. No doubt about it. The police are really digging in. The story doesn't quite say so but I think they are working on a couple of very promising leads."

"I'm sorry but I don't know----"

"Today's Times. Metro section. Page B2. Left hand column. You really ought to read it."

She half smiles again. "I'm sorry. I see someone I really must talk to."

"I can't imagine which is worse. Believing that she killed herself or learning that she was murdered in cold blood by someone close to her."

"Both equally abhorrent," she says as she starts off. I subtly block her way.

"I guess now that Virginia's gone, that would make you sole heir to your mother's estate."

"Does it? I hadn't given it any thought," she lies.

"Not that it's important. One look at this terrific setup you have here and anyone can tell that money is secondary."

"Quite right, Mr. Bernardi, and now if---"

"But then again with the vagaries of the art world, one never knows where one stands. One decade it's Picasso, the next it's Jackson Pollock or say, Lazslo D'Allesandro. It never hurts to have a pile of rainy day money, wouldn't you say, Miss Jenks?"

"I would say, Mr. Bernardi, that your behavior is boorish. Please excuse me. Lazslo." She walks off leading Lazslo by the hand. He smiles at me as he walks by.

"Hoppy to mitt you," he says.

Hoppy to mitt you, too, old chum, I think, as I go in search of Bunny.

I scour the first floor. No sign of her. There's a bar set up near the staircase and I belly my way politely to an empty space next to Nigel Bruce and his wife Violet. The bartender smiles politely. I ask for a beer. He offers wine. Red, white or rose. I smile back and edge away. To me wine is a waste of a good bunch of grapes.

I start to climb the stairs when I spot Eddie Robinson entering by himself. Gladys apparently decided to stay home making her wiser than most of us. Robinson looks around, walks over to a painting and gives it a quick look. He then heads toward the jock strop guy with the cat and gives it maybe five seconds. I see him shake his head and then he turns and leaves. I have heard that Robinson knows art like Culbertson knows bridge. I think maybe Lazslo doesn't have much of a future in the art game.

Bunny's upstairs, backed against the wall by a young guy in a tux and a bad case of teenage acne. He has his hand on her hip only inches from her luscious backside. I firmly take his hand and remove it as I smile congenially.

"Mine," I say.

"Sorry, sir," he says, his voice cracking. He slinks off in search of other prey. Does his babysitter know he's escaped out the backdoor?

"Cute guy," I say to Bunny.

"His name is Harvey. He graduates next month," she says.

"Made it all the way to ninth grade, did he? Good for him."

"Don't be snide."

"Merely jealous."

"That's all right, then," she says. "How'd it go with Olivia?"

"She could hardly bear to tear herself away from me."

"Does that mean we can now exit these premises?"

"It does."

We head for the stairs and start down. On the way we pass Mona Freeman coming up. I lean in and whisper "Beware of Harvey." She looks at me oddly. She doesn't get it, but she will.

As we reach the landing a strange little man steps in front of us, blocking our way.

"Mr. Bernardi?" he asks pleasantly.

I confess that I am.

"Daniel David Doyle," he says, offering a thin, well manicured hand. "Phineas Ogilvy sends his regards."

Immediately I know who this guy is. He's the Times art critic and according to Phineas, a good man to know and far from the dapper fop his readers believe him to be.

We shake. I introduce Bunny. He is gallant and complimentary. The room is getting crowded. People are trying to get upstairs. We move to one side to make room.

"Do you have a few minutes? Phineas thought I might be of some service to you."

"Sure," I say.

Bunny says, "You two talk. I'm going to take another look at that painting." She goes off to reassess the guy in the jock strop. Daniel David Doyle takes me by the elbow and leads me off into a corner where it is quieter.

Doyle is a little man. Five-three, maybe, and elegantly dressed in a cashmere jacket, silk shirt, sunflower yellow ascot. His shoes are highly polished and he wears spats. He takes out a silver cigarette holder, offers me a cigarette and after I refuse, he lights up.

"I presume you've met Olivia," he says.

I nod. "And chatted with her."

"And did you also chat wth Lazslo D'Allesandro?" he asks imitatively, sounding more like Bela Lugosi than Lugosi himself.

"Oh, does he chat?"

"Not that you would notice," Doyle says. "So Olivia is the surviving sibling. Someday that will make her a very rich woman."

"I surmised as much," I say.

"I don't know how much you know about the Jenks family and the dynamics of their relationships but Phineas felt you ought to be informed and who better to educate you than me?"

"I'm grateful."

"The old man was a lumber baron in Oregon, leased thousands of acres of timber land, started six lumber mills throughout the state and when he was thirty six years old, sold everything for about twenty million dollars.

"He came to Los Angeles to find a wife and settle down which he did. In two years he had two daughters. After that he lost interest in progeny. During the war he invested wisely and became even richer. In '44 when he keeled over of a heart attack he was said to be worth nearly forty million dollars."

"Impressive."

"His widow Lucretia was so shattered, she took to her bed and shut herself off from the world. At first it was all mental but after two years of inactivity and abusing all sorts of quack medicines, she actually became disabled. A couple of strokes ensued and these days she leaves her bedroom only rarely. Meanwhile Olivia and the prince consort wait for the inevitable."

"Alexander Farnsworth. I've met him."

"Slick as bacon grease on a kitchen floor," Doyle says.

"Yes, I shook his hand once."

Doyle smiles and then looks around, taking in the glitzy ambience. "As for all this," he says, "it's papier mache. If the old lady hadn't started pumping money into it a few months back, today it would be a flower shop."

"Making Virginia's death all the more interesting from a financial point of view."

"Precisely."

"And so the odds of Olivia making it on her own without Mama's help---"

"Are about the same as Lazslo D'Allesandro selling even one painting to this assemblage of nitwits," Doyle says. He hesitates, screwing up his face. "No, wait. I take that back. There is a chance, slight though it may be, that this place is not headed for the graveyard. In the past two weeks they've acquired a Toulouse-Lautrec and a previously unknown Hals. Probably cost them a fortune and God knows where they got the cash, but if they can turn them over for a fast profit, they might keep the doors open.

"Might?"

"Might. My money's still on bankruptcy," Doyle says.

I put out my hand.

"Thank you for your valuable insight, Mr. Doyle. It's been a delight to meet you."

"Thank you," he smiles. "Now I must seek out our hostess and tell her how excited I am to be here."

He walks off and I catch up with Bunny who is again staring quizzically at the painting.

"Sixty five hundred dollars," she says.

I nod. "It would look good in the bathroom."

She also nods. "It would," she agrees.

"Does that price include the frame?" I ask.

"No."

"Then to hell with it. No frame, no sale."

And we leave for home where we have better things to do.

CHAPTER FOURTEEN

undays are special. The alarm clock has been disabled. The shades have been drawn the night before so no early morning sun can trouble our sleep. If we're lucky we won't stir until well past nine o'clock. Usually it's me that first slithers out of bed and into the bathroom. Half awake I will go to the kitchen and make a pot of coffee, then go to the front door to retrieve the Sunday L.A. Times which I will plop down on the kitchen table. By this time the aroma of brewing coffee has pervaded the bedroom and Bunny will appear, hair looking like a fright wig from 'Return of the Cat People', makeupless, wearing a shapeless garment only one generation removed from a flour sack. Silently she will find a coffee cup, pour herself some joe and without a word, return to the bedroom. If I am lucky she will reappear about an hour later looking somewhat more presentable.

I will fix myself some breakfast. Usually toast, juice and coffee, sometimes bacon and eggs, and only rarely french toast which I have not yet mastered. I will read the paper starting with the sports section. When Bunny appears she will grab Style and Fashion. I will start on the crossword puzzle.She will start looking at the listings for houses for sale. Not that she intends to buy, she just likes to fantasize.

Around two we walk down to the nearby Howard Johnson's for lunch. When we get back we curl up in the living room and go at the paper again. That or a good book. Sometimes we fall asleep. Amend that. Sometimes I fall asleep. Somewhere near seven we break out a can of Campbell's soup and apple pie and settle down to watch the Sunday night schedule. When Ed Sullivan is done, so are we. We retire to the bedroom where I am always dismayed to find that no one has made the bed from the night before. We either make mad passionate love or we read some more, depending upon how exhausted we are from our day's activities. Lights out at ten. Tomorrow is another day.

This Sunday, however, is not destined to be quite so peaceful.

The phone rings at 8:30. I am furious. Don't they know what day it is?

"Hello," I growl.

"Did I wake you? Sorry."

"Who is this?"

"Aaron Kleinschmidt."

"Who died?"

"Nobody. Are you awake enough to listen carefully?"

"I can try."

"Good. Ten o'clock this morning. Forest Lawn Cemetery They're exhuming the body of Leon Schroeder."

"What? Why?"

"Looking for poison."

"What for? Doesn't that crazy wife know that Virginia is dead?"

"Don't ask me intelligent questions. I'm just the messenger. Thought you'd like to know."

"Actually, I do," I say. "You got your boy for the weekend?" Kleinschmidt's divorced and only a parttime father.

"I do." he says. "We're going to tackle the Santa Monica Pier."

"Always fun.Tell him hi for me and thanks again for the call, Sarge."

"Let me know if anything interesting happens out there," he says.

"I'll do that."

I hang up and pad my way into the bathroom in search of a razor and a toothbrush. Bunny is still asleep. I'm going to leave her that way.

By the time I turn into the entrance of the cemetery, it's ten past ten. I'm ready to ask directions but before I can stop at the main office, a squad car flies past me and heads up the road to the left. On a hunch I follow and several hundred yards up the road, across from the Wee Kirk Church, I see a handful of cars, a coroner's van and a backhoe hard at work. I get close and pull to the side of the road. Up ahead, standing by their parked car, I see Emma Schroeder and Harlow Quinn, the Assistant D.A. He has his arm around her in a comforting fashion. Exhumation is not an every day occurence. I see now how this one was so readily ordered up.

As I near the scene, a uniformed policeman steps into my path holding up his hand. "Excuse me, sir, this is official county business."

I nod and lean in close. "Sergeant Kleinschmidt called me earlier this morning," I say out of the corner of my mouth.

"Are you family?"

"Spiritual advisor," I say.

He mulls that over for a moment and then lets me pass. I thank him and continue on.

Emma Schroeder is the first to see me coming and she is none too thrilled. She leans over and whispers something into Quinn's ear. He looks at me coming and then steps forward to intercept me.

"What are you doing here, Mr. Bernardi?" he asks.

"I was notified by the police," I say.

He frowns. "Why?"

"Beats me," I say. I look over at Emma. "How's the grieving widow holding up?"

"I really don't think you belong here," Quinn says.

"Probably not," I say, "but when the stiff in the box steals my life's work and then up and dies on me before I can kick his teeth in, I make it my business to find out what's going on." I am deliberately crude because I want to spark a reaction. Nice Nellies get treated like Nice Nellies. I want to be treated like a belligerent guy with no couth.

"I think you'd better leave," he says.

"Since your gal pal thinks her husband was murdered by Virginia Jenks and Virginia Jenks is dead and beyond the reach of the justice system, could you tell me what this exercise is all about?"

"No offense but I'm going to have you removed." He starts toward the security cop.

"Hah. I knew it," I say. "Something to hide. Can't wait to pass this along to my pal Lou Cioffi at the Times. He's already intrigued about this whole business." I gamble that as an Assistant D.A. he knows who Cioffi is and has probably read the story in yesterday's paper. It turns out I'm right.

"Now just a moment," Quinn says. "Emma had nothing to do with that woman's death."

"And I'd be more apt to believe that if you weren't treating me like a leper come to join you for Thanksgiving dinner."

He hesitates. I look past him. The backhoe is quiet. Now guys with shovels are hopping into the grave to finish the job. Quinn takes a quick look in Emma's direction and then he says, "It's about the money."

"Thirty-five thousand dollars."

"That's right. Emma believes that the insurance payout is rightly hers as his wife. The company disagrees. Emma believes that if she can show that Virginia poisoned Leon, the insurance company will disqualify her as the beneficiary. Instead of Virginia's heirs getting the money, it will go to Emma."

"Then there was nothing vindictive about it?" I say.

"Vindictive? No, why should there be?"

"Oh, I don't know," I say offhandedly. "An attractive woman like Emma loses her husband to a plain Jane like Virginia. Might have raised a jealous hackle or two."

"Surely that's not a motive for murder."

"Then pile on the loss of a huge insurance settlement. Had to be infuriating."

"You're way off base here, Mr. Bernardi. Emma is no killer. I promise you that."

I shake my head in mock disgust. "Oh, you lawyers are all alike. That's all we ever hear. Promises, promises."

"No doubt you think you're funny," Quinn says to me.

"Funny? No," I say. "The cops tell me I'm no longer under suspicion but you know what I think? I think I was the last person to see her alive about twenty minutes before she's found dead and I have one helluva motive for killing her and when they finally realize that they can't figure out what happened, they may come back and give me a real hard look. So, funny? I hardly think so."

"My condolences. Sometimes life is tough," Quinn says with just the right amount of nastiness.

"You know, Harlow. I understand where Emma fits into all this. What I don't get is you. I took the time to check. You're a married man."

"If you'd really checked, Bernardi, you'd have found that my wife and I have been separated for months and she is filing for divorce."

"Clearing the way for Emma to become the next Mrs. Quinn."

"I don't know. I haven't asked her."

"A formality. You seem very much in love, Harlow. I guess you'd do just about anything for her. And I mean anything,"

"I don't like that insinuation."

"Don't be so touchy, Harlow. I was referring to that." I point to the exhumation process. "That's not cheap and I doubt it's ever done on a whim. You seem to have the District Attorney's utmost confidence."

"I do and always have. And, incidentally, only my friends call me Harlow," he says.

"I'll try to remember that." I smile. "Well, thanks for your time. I could be all wet, you know. I'm just reflecting what others are thinking. You wouldn't be the first guy vamped into doing something stupid by some beautiful dame. Have you ever read James M. Cain? 'Double Indemnity'. 'The Postman Always Rings Twice'. Oh, never mind. It's not important. Let me know the results of the new autopsy. I'm very curious. And don't forget to send me an invitation to the wedding. I'm a sucker for a love story with a happy ending."

I turn and head back to my car. I can feel his eyes boring into my back. No matter. I feel great. This has been an excellent weekend. I have poked away at Emma and her boyfriend, at Olivia and by extension, her boyfriend Alex as well. Lou Cioffi thinks he's onto the story of the year and may already be smelling Pulitzer. There is only one more person I have yet to harrass and miracle of miracles, even as I think it, the snazzy DeSoto pulls up and parks behind me.

The lady in the silly hats gets out. This morning Charlotte Schroeder is wearing a man's derby with a huge orange and yellow feather jammed into the ribbon that surrounds the crown. If this were Peru, it would be considered high fashion.

I step in front of her and smile, extending my hand.

"Mrs. Schroeder? Joseph Bernardi," I say.

She takes it uncertainly and briefly nods her head.

"How do you do."

"My deepest sympathies on your loss, Mrs. Schroeder, and even more so because of the appalling procedure occurring here."

"Thank you."

"You must be devastated, losing Leon at such a young age, and then the terrible tragedy of Virginia's death."

"One bears up, Mr.--uh---" Her eyes narrow suspiciously.

"Bernardi. Joseph Bernardi."

"Are you a reporter, sir?"

"I am not, ma'am. I work for Warner Brothers Studios."

She nods her head in understanding. "Yes, you'd be the young man who claims that Virginia stole your novel."

"You are well informed," I say.

"Virginia had no secrets from me."

"You were close, then," I say.

"Very." She smiles. "I know that probably sounds odd to you considering all this---" She waves her hand in the direction of the backhoe. "---this nonsense," she continues, "because that's what it is, you know. Total fabricated nonsense coming from a spiteful woman who trapped my boy into a loveless marriage and never gave him a moment's peace."

"That's quite an accusation," I say.

"And every word of it true," she says sharply. She's getting agitated. I can see it in her eyes. "Emma was not worthy of my son. He was special. Oh, yes, very special but she treated him like dirt. All she wanted from him was the money. Money for clothes and for jewelry and fancy clothes. Leon made an excellent living, you know. He wrote jingles and slogans for an advertising agency. Free lance, of course. I had told him, do not get tied down. Be your own person. He listened to me, young man. He always listened to me. Or he did until that woman came along. It was Emma, always Emma. I could have killed her." She sees the look on my face. "Oh, good God, I didn't mean that literally. And then one day, I guess she went too far even for Leon and he left her and came back to me."

"And left right away again for Virginia," I say.

She looks at me sharply. "Don't, Mr. Bernardi. You don't know what you're talking about. Virginia was real and genuine. Only when he met Virginia did Leon start to enjoy real happiness in his life."

"Yes, she was that kind of person," I say.

"Indeed, she was. She tried very hard to bring out the best in him. She was quiet and subtle but she was effective. I could see it on his face and hear it in his voice. She was making a man out of him."

"He was an only child, I believe."

"He was," she says. "Mr. Schroeder and I were young when we married. After Leon was born he realized his mistake and walked away but in doing so, he started sending me a check every month for my care and the care of the boy. Those checks continue to this day even though I haven't seen the man in twenty seven years."

"Sad," I say, "but at least you had Leon."

"It was not sad, sir, and yes, I had Leon and I still had him, even on a sharing basis, right up until the day he died." She takes a couple of steps in the direction of the exhumation and her eyes are hard as black marbles. "I wish I had the courage and the wherewithal to do something about that heartless bitch." She turns to me. "You will forgive my language, Mr. Bernardi."

"Of course."

"I am not usually so intemperate." She throws one last look in the direction of Emma and Alex. "I think I've seen quite enough of this," she says. She puts out her hand which I take. "So nice to meet you, Mr. Bernardi."

"It's mutual, Mrs. Schroeder," I say.

I watch as she gets back in her car and drives off. I take one last look at the site. The workers are now pulling the coffin from the grave. Leon Schroeder will have to endure one more indignity before they give him any peace. I wonder what kind of a man he really was. I can no longer regard him as evil. Yes, he stole my work, but I think what he wanted most, what he desperately needed, was to find a place for himself, to make a mark that said 'Leon Schroeder was here'. The way he chose was unwise and in the end, he died anonymously, unknown to anyone except the very few that loved him most.

I drive away with a heavy heart. I am praying that Emma and Alex find no poison with which to besmirch Virginia's name. She, too, deserved better in this lifetime.

CHAPTER FIFTEEN

'm at the studio early Monday morning and looking for Henry Blanke who is not only a good producer but a good friend as well. We got close in Mexico during location shooting in Tampico and he's made it clear his door is always open to me for any reason. These days he's very busy getting 'Bright Leaf' ready for release in early July and half the time he's out of the office or worse, out of town. This morning I get lucky. He's coming up the stairs as I'm coming down. Does he have a minute? For me? Ja. He's been living here for decades but every once in a while, his German heritage breaks out.

"So, Joe, what can I do for you?" he asks as he settles down behind his desk which is piled high with scripts, paperwork and correspondence.

I tell him my sad story of hard work, pride in what I've written and anger over betrayal. I make sure he understands that RKO was very interested in the copycat version as was a publishing house. Corporate cowardice has made them back off. I hope for a braver reaction from Warners.

He nods. "I will be honored to read your book, Joe. And I am flattered you thought of me. But I will be honest. I am buried under a pile of projects. My next two films are already set in stone. Nonetheless, if your work has merit, I will support it in every way."

I tell him I could not be more grateful and leave behind a copy of my book which he places on top of the stack of scripts waiting to be read. I realize I am probably playing my last card. If Henry backs away, I doubt I have anywhere else to go. We shake hands and I head back to my office. Reality is setting in. Novel writing is about a lot more than just story telling. It is a gauntlet of uncertainties and as nerve wracking as walking a high wire without a net.

When I walk into my office, Glenda Mae tells me I had an urgent phone call from someone named Oswald Pennybaker. He left a number. I ask her to get him for me.

"Oswald. Joe Bernardi."

"Thanks for getting back right away," he says. "How's your morning look?"

"Nothing important."

"Good. Eleven o'clock. A memorial service for Virginia at the Chapel of the Pines Crematorium. Anybody who's anybody will be there including Mother Jenks. Thought you'd like to know."

"You're right. Where is this place?" I ask. He tells me. "I'll see you there just before eleven."

At ten of eleven I swing onto Catalina Street and there it is, up ahead. It looks more like an observatory than a crematorium but in Los Angeles, architecture is a matter of taste. Mostly bad. I pull into the parking area a few feet from an oversized unmarked white van. The driver, dressed all in white, is standing by.

Oswald is waiting for me by the front entrance puffing on a cigarette. He takes one last deep drag and ditches it as I approach.

"The gang's all here," he says.

I nod toward the van. "So I see. What's that, some kind of ambulance?"

"A clinic on wheels. Everything you might need at a moment's notice. The driver's name is Al. Chatty sort. He's also a registered nurse. When Mother Jenks goes out and about, which isn't often, this is how she travels."

I nod appreciatively. "Nice to have money," I say.

"I wouldn't know," Oswald says.

"I'm surprised that the coroner released the body so quickly."

"A lot of pressure there. But he got everything he needed. So did forensics. By the way, just so you know, the print guy picked up four sets of prints throughout the entire bungalow. Mine and Virginia's for sure. I'm betting the other two are Maybelle Ruskin and Charlotte Schroeder. Those are the only two I ever saw enter her place."

"Not hard to pick that lock," I say.

"No, and rubber gloves are forty cents a pair at Woolworth's."

Oswald and I open the crematorium door. Soft, mournful organ music floats toward us. I smell gardenias. Off to the left is a door that opens onto a small chapel. A placard by the door reads 'Jenks Memorial'.

We slip into the back pew. Up front is a small raised altar with a lectern. Behind it a colorful stained glass window. In the middle of the aisle on a gurney is a coffin, draped in silk. I learn later that the coffin was a plain pine box. In a crematorium you try not to set fire to walnut or mahogany. Sitting in the first pew are Olivia and Alex and an older white-haired woman hunched over with scoliosis and with tubes in her nose which are attached to an oxygen tank at her side. Sitting beside her is an older gentleman. Only if he were wearing his stethoscope would it be easier to identify him as her doctor.

In the second row are Maybelle Ruskin and Charlotte Schroeder and the Jabberwocky owner, Bahadur Singh. Scattered behind them in the next several rows are a couple of dozen men and women, many of whom I recognize from the reading Bunny and I attended.

The music, which is obviously recorded and piped in through strategically placed speakers, stops. A solemn looking gentleman in a black suit moves to the lectern, quietly recounts Virginia's many gentle and loving traits and then steps aside to make room for a heavy set man in three-piece grey with a solid black silk tie. I cannot remember his name but he is an actor and he proves it when mellifluous tones begin to emanate from his mouth. He is apparently reading one of Virginia's better known poems. He may be getting paid for this, maybe not, but the words make no more sense coming from him than they did from Virginia. Or maybe someone smarter than me can explain what a dust-encrusted windmill of galactic resonance is.

The service done with, Oswald and I are the first ones outside where Oswald lights up another cigarette.

"They say those things will kill you," I say.

"My doctor told me that twenty years ago and here I am 83 years old and still ambulatory."

I nod. "Point taken. And what's your doctor say now?"

"Not much. He died. Only 52 years old. A real shame."

"I'd say so. What did he died of?"

"Too much exercise. Went out for a six mile run one day and his heart just quit on him. I'm telling you, son, you only get one heart. You gotta take care of it."

The others are all exiting now and the final group to come through the door is Mother Jenks in a wheelchair being pushed by her doctor followed by Olivia and Alex. I start forward hoping for a few words with the old lady but Alex is quicker than I am and he cuts me off. He smiles for the benefit of the crowd but his words are razor-edged.

"Don't even think of it," he says.

"I merely want to pay my respects to Virginia's mother," I say.

"Yes, Olivia told me how you paid respects on Saturday evening at the gallery. Take a hint, bud. You're in the wrong place and you're playing the wrong game."

"Just trying to get some answers."

"Haven't got any. Neither does Olivia. Now stay out of the way before your curiosity gets you into quicksand you can't get out of."

"Alex, please. Tell me that's not a threat."

"I will tell you that your life will be much simpler, much quieter and very much safer if you return to your studio and go back to puffing up your second rate movies."

"Well, now you've hurt my feelings," I say."Have you seen 'The Damned Don't Cry' with Joan Crawford? Just came out last weekend. Nothing second rate about it."

He fails to smile. "Goodbye, Mr. Bernardi. And take me seriously. I'm a serious guy."

He turns on his heel and catches up with Olivia and her mother at the van. The rear doors are open and they are preparing to load the old woman in on a hydraulic lift. Oswald sidles up next to me.

"Young Farnsworth seemed out of sorts," he comments.

"He hasn't been sleeping well. I think it's made him cranky," I say.

"Word of advice, Joe. Never underestimate a man carrying a gun."

I look back toward him sharply. "He's packing?"

Oswald nods. "Small caliber. Maybe a thirty-two in a holster in the small of his back."

"How long did you say you'd been a police chief?"

"Long enough," he replies.

I'm back at the office by one o'clock with a ham and swiss I picked up at a deli. I'll eat in, read the trades and maybe even doze off for a half hour if the mood strikes me. My head is reeling as I contemplate what I have done the past couple of days. I have picked a quarrel with Olivia Jenks and an Assistant District Attorney, subtly grilled a grieving mother, and sloughed off a slick con man who has plans to marry into the Jenks fortune. I have not only asked for trouble, I seem to have begged for it. For the first time I realize that roiling snakes carries with it a certain amount of danger.

Glenda Mae's gone out for lunch and I'm in the anteroom pouring myself a cup of coffee when Kirk Douglas walks into the office. He tosses me a big smile.

"Joe, how goes it?" he asks.

"Busy, Kirk," I say. "They're coming at me from all sides."

"Well, not me, pal," he says and then frowns. "And what the hell is that?" he asks peering into my coffee cup.

"Best coffee in the studio," I tell him.

"Looks like coal tar," he says.

"Take a sip," I say, pouring some into fresh cup and handing it to him. He shrugs and sips. He smiles appeciatively. "Hey. that's pretty good. What's that flavor? There's something extra in this."

"Chickory. It grows wild down south."

"Sorry. I'm just a poor kid from Amsterdam, New York. We don't know from such things but I'll tell Diana to get some in. Yeah, it's good, Joe. Very good."

"So are you looking forward to the picture?"

"You bet. It'll be great working with Art Kennedy again and I hear Jane Wyman's a peach."

"You heard right."

"Don't know much about Gertrude Lawrence but I guess she'll be okay," he says.

"I'm sure she wlll," I say.

"Look, I'm going to be out camping with the family for the next couple of weeks so I'm just checking in now to see if there's anything you need from me before I disappear."

"Can't think of anything," I say. "I've got tons of glossies and I'll write a couple of 'Kirk says' releases. The usual glop."

"Great," he says. "Listen, just one thing. The part of Tom is just terrific and Art Kennedy's going to be superb, I know it. The role was made for him so when you start drumbeating, see what you can do about stirring up some Oscar talk for him."

"I'll do what I can."

"He really got screwed on 'Champion'. I mean, Jagger's a nice old guy and he was good but Art was fresh and dynamic, you know what I mean?"

"I do."

"Maybe the Hollywood old boys gave it to Jagger out of sentiment. Okay, so be it. But Art's got another chance here and I'd like to see him rewarded."

"How about Kirk Douglas? You think he should be rewarded?" I ask.

He laughs. "Me? Naw. Brod Crawford deserved it last year. He was just terrific. If I hadn't been nominated he would have gotten my vote."

"And Glass Menagerie?"

"No," he says, "the part's not there. There'll be something

else down the line. I'll wait my turn." He checks his watch. "Oops, gotta run. Don't forget. Big push for Art."

"I'll remember," I say as he heads out the door and down the corridor to the stairwell.

I warm up my coffee and go back into my office. The trades are still laid out neatly as is the morning Times. I pick up The Reporter and I think of Bunny. I wonder if she's heard from Walt Davenport and if she has, I wonder what she's told him. I guess I'll find out soon enough. I try to put it out of my mind.

My thoughts turn back to Virginia's death. I know my next move but it will have to keep until lunch hour is over. Since we're talking about Phineas Ogilvy, who never met a quiche he couldn't savor, this probably means a wait until at least three o'clock. Just then the phone rings. I pick up.

"Bernardi."

"Joe, it's Tom." I'm silent for a moment. Tom who?

"Tom Williams, my friend. Playwright, screenwriter, all round bon vivant."

It comes to me.

"How's Key West?"

"Nothing could be fina---" he says, recalling the old song. "Joe, our local paper picked up one of your releases this morning. I was liberally quoted."

"Sorry if you're upset, Tom, but you know how the game is played."

"Upset? No, no. Not in the least. I was highly amused. Even more so after having received the latest changes to the script written by my co-screenwriter 'what's-his-name'." Tennessee knows his name and so do I but we just don't acknowledge it.

"Would you like to hear what I really think about the script, the role and Miss Lawrence? I'd be delighted to fill you in, NOT for publication, of course."

146

"You have my total attention," I tell him.

"You will remember our last conversation."

"Vividly."

"The part of Amanda has now been rewritten and padded to give Miss Lawrence added screen time. While dear Laurette Taylor made my Broadway Amanda tender and radiant, the film Amanda will be a burlesque queen, played for laughs. with none of the reality needed to bolster the story's framework. Now I may be selling Miss Lawrence short. Maybe she has the chops to find some sort of reality in this female grotesquery though I doubt it. The impetus for these alterations came from one of two sources, Miss Lawrence herself or Mr. Warner, that paragon of good taste and intellectual honesty."

"If you're asking me, I don't know," I say.

"I have heard it rumored that Lord Jack is hoping for an Oscar for this film. He can hope all he likes. The critics, while often fools, are not totally stupid and neither are the Academy voters. The Menagerie will end up being nothing but a pile of shattered glass. Now, Joe, have you written all this down?"

"No," I say.

"Good," Tennessee replies. "I am expecting my final check from your business office and I would hate to see something happen to it. Til later, then, my friend," And he hangs up.

I look over to the side of my desk and sitting there, atop a pile of correspondence, is the revised script for 'The Glass Menagerie'. Jane Wyman and Gertrude Lawrence both expect me whip up an Oscar for them and I am terrified to read this new script.

Just when you thought you didn't have enough to worry about.

CHAPTER SIXTEEN

It's five o'clock. We're gathered in Lou Cioffi's cramped office on the second floor of the Times building. He rates an office because he is technically the assistant editor of the Metro section in addition to being the paper's leading crime reporter. At my request, Phineas put this meeting together. The purpose is to use Lou's stories to put increasing pressure on Virginia's killer. It may require a little manipulation of the truth. That's why Phineas is there and why I brought along Oswald Pennybaker who spent decades up north dealing with the press, often joining forces with local reporters to ferret out wrongdoers.

"Let me get this straight," Lou is saying. "You want a major story on this, a full court press, mostly facts and a few embellishments thrown in for dramatic effect."

"That's about it," I say.

"In other words, you want me to print lies," he says.

"No, no," Phineas breaks in. "We want to touch on facts as yet unproven. Educated hypotheses. Truths yet to be uncovered."

"Lies," Lou insists.

"That's such a harsh word," Phineas laments.

"Look, Lou," I say, "most of what we want you to cover is

public knowledge and provable. Around the edges it's a little hypothetical but also sensible and highly probable."

"You want me to strongly hint that Olivia Jenks aced her sister to collect the entire inheritance, not just half, which she and the boyfriend will need to keep the art gallery afloat. Is that about it?"

"Close enough," I say.

Oswald jumps in. "It's not a crime, Mr. Cioffi. If you phrase it properly it's not even libel. I used the press often back in Ukiah when I knew I was onto something. It almost always worked out."

Lou smiles mirthlessly. "I like that word 'almost'."

"We've got Doyle's information, that the gallery is teetering on bankruptcy and that the mother is refusing to put any more money into the venture."

"Hearsay and rumors," Lou says.

"Yeah, but you know it's true," I say. "Look, it's not like we're just picking on Olivia and Alex here. There are other people who stood to gain from Virginia's death."

"Who and how?" he asks.

"Emma Schroeder, for one. Thirty five thousand dollars worth of insurance money is a lot of motive."

Lou holds up a finger. "Okay, that's one."

"Maybelle Ruskin for two, Mr. Cioffi," Oswald breaks in.

"Her agent? Are you kidding me? What does she get out of it?"

"Have you checked with the coroner's office lately?" Oswald asks him.

"No."

"You should. The revised autopsy confirms the original. Leon Schroeder's remains reveal no poison in his system."

"So?"

"That means the insurance payoff will go to Virginia's heirs and except for a token $5,000 bequest to me, the balance of her estate---everything--- goes to her agent, Maybelle Ruskin."

Lou leans back in his chair. "You're well informed, Mr. Pennybaker. I'm surprised." So am I but I don't say so.

Oswald smiles. "I have many friends in the department," he says. "Some I've known for nearly twenty years."

Lou looks around the room skeptically, clicking and unclicking a well worn Zippo cigarette lighter. Then he reaches into a huge glass jar on his desk and takes out a baby blue bubble gum ball and starts chewing on it furiously. He looks down at his desk top. His jaws keep working. An ex-smoker if I ever saw one. Then he looks up.

"Okay, suppose I do this. My feeling is we make it really big. Impossible to ignore. So big that if there's blowback people will start to wonder what someone might be hiding." He looks at me. "Joe?"

"Yes, it's the way to go."

"I'm gonna need quotes from a well known local poet who will expound on the lady's talent, the great loss we've all suffered. the world is now a poorer place, yak, yak, yak." He looks around the room.

"I know someone," Phineas says. "Jesse T. Humphreys. He has an excellent reputation and is published, but he's poor as a churchmouse. I think he'd do it if he understood what we were up to and also if we threw in a hundred dollars."

"That's no problem," Lou says. "What do we do about Sergeant Califano?"

"Spread his name around the story liberally," I say. "He's hardworking, tenacious, a bulldog, won't give up easily. Paint him as a good guy."

"Get a quote?" Lou asks.

"No. Surprise him," I say.

"What about the suspects?" Phineas asks.

"Wait until minutes before press time, give them a chance to comment and print what they have to say. If we can't reach them---" Lou shrugs. "---well, too bad. We tried."

"You'll want to plaster this story with pictures," I say. "You've probably got file photos on Olivia and D.A. Quinn. Maybelle maybe. I'd check the morgue for anything on Alex Farnsworth. Also check the cops. Something tells me he's got a sheet."

Lou nods. "Anything we haven't thought of?"

"Prayer," Oswald says dryly.

On that there is total agreement.

I head back to the office to check in just in case a fire needs extinguishing. Funny how crises always seem to pop up at day's end. I park and just as I am getting out of my car, I hear my name being shouted and I look up. Charlie Berger is leaning out of his window and waving for me to come up to his office.

He greets me at his door holding a covered platter.

"Is there some reason why Eleanor Parker should be sending me a spinach quiche with a huge thank you note along with it?"

I laugh and explain what's going on. I've already coordinated with Pathe News who will be at Bert and Eleanor's house on Friday to shoot some newsreel footage. Buddy Raskin, my favorite photographer will be on hand shooting color and black and white for a spread in 'Redbook'. The magazine will be supplying its own reporter.

Charlie nods. "Sounds okay," he says. "Probably Bert's idea."

"It is," I say.

He looks down at the platter dolefully.

"I hate quiche," he says. "So does my secretary."

I put out my hands. "I know just the place for it," I say. I take it from him and head down the hallway to my office. By now I have figured out that Beau will eat anything provided it's not moving. Glenda Mae will be so pleased. But when I get to my office she has left for the day. I put the quiche in the office refrigerator. She can be pleased tomorrow. I close up and head for home.

I swing into the driveway about quarter past six expecting to see Bunny home ahead of me. Then I remember she had to attend some press conference at five o'clock at CBS Columbia Square on Sunset Boulevard. Something about making a TV version of Lucille Ball's radio show, 'My Favorite Husband' with Lucy and her real life husband Desi Arnaz. I'm not sure about any of this. When people start talking about television production, even darling Bunny, I tune out.

Since I'm first home, I rummage around in the refrigerator for anything that looks like it might be dinner. I spot an unopened package of frankfurters in the bottom shelf and I know we have a jar of sauerkraut in the pantry. I also find a can of Boston baked beans. Not gourmet and not very inventive but it'll do and it won't take long to whip up. I lay everything out and flip on the TV in the living room to the local news. There's not much of interest. A couple of car accidents, a city councilman's wife died after a long illness, three teenagers were caught shoplifting at the May Company, and somebody important retired from the county Sheriff's Department. Before my eyelids can droop to half mast, Bunny comes bounding in the kitchen door. I greet her with a kiss. When I see she is carrying a six pack of Coors and a chocolate cream pie from the bakery, I give her another kiss. Any excuse will do.

I open two of the beers and hand her one as she sits at the

kitchen table and slips off her shoes. I take out a small saucepan and fill it halfway with water and put some heat under it. When it starts to boil I'll toss in four of the frankfurters. As I set the table I ask her how the press conference went. She laughs.

"Everything you heard is true," she says.

"I didn't hear anything. I'm in the movie business."

"Lucy's quitting her radio show to go into television."

"Now that I did hear," I say.

"I can't believe it," she says. "With her Hooper ratings, she must be crazy. And Desi playing her husband? My God."

"He IS her husband," I remind her.

"Sure, in real life but it'll never work on television."

I shrug. "CBS must think it'll work."

She shakes her head. "CBS doesn't know what to think except that Lucy has a lot of clout. You know what they're going to do? They're going to write two or three episodes and then play them live at theaters up and down the coast to see how the audiences react. Just like the Marx Brothers used to do when they had a script for a new movie."

"You're kidding."

"Nope. If I read it right I think CBS insisted on it. Guess they figure Desi will fall flat on his ass and Lucy'll come to her senses and go back to the radio show."

"Knowing Lucy, there's little chance of that."

"My thoughts exactly," Bunny says.

We're laughing and scratching and having an amiable time but through it all there's an undercurrent and the undercurrent has to do with a phone call that Walter Davenport was supposed to have made some time today.

There's a lull in the conversation and Bunny takes advantage of it by telling me, "I didn't talk to Walt today. He got called to

Washington. Something important, according to his secretary. Something about Korea."

And even as she says it I can hear the voice of Douglas Edwards, the CBS news reporter, coming from the living room. I walk in with Bunny following me and we stare at the television. Edwards is looking solemn and there is a map of Korea on the screen behind him.

".......a half dozen incursions by North Korean troops across the 38th parallel in the past two days. Shots have been fired by both sides but there are no known casualties. In the face of this deliberate provocation, South Korean forces have cancelled all leaves and beefed up security all along the border. A spokesman for Secretary of State Dean Acheson describes the situation as grave. There is concern throughout Washington that the slightest miscalculation by either the North or the South could plunge the peninsula into all out war."

Bunny and I look at one another. I sag down onto the couch, suddenly frightened and praying that this crisis will blow over. We have just endured a horrific war. We should not have to deal with another one.

Meanwhile in the kitchen water continues to boil and four cold frankfurters lay untouched on the kitchen counter.

CHAPTER SEVENTEEN

WHO KILLED VIRGINIA JENKS?

That's the headline.

PROMISING POETESS CUT DOWN IN PRIME OF LIFE

And that's the sub-head.

As promised, the story is major. It runs on page 5 and takes up every inch of space. It features photos of all the principals. Olivia and Alex are mugging for the camera at the art gallery several months ago. Charlotte Schroeder, in a silly hat, is shown at a social event, her face probably cropped from a photo that included others. Maybelle's is a professional glossy probably taken when she opened her agency. The shot of Emma Schroeder was taken at a news conference where she is flanked by Assistant District Attorney Harlow Quinn. Even Oswald gets his moment of notoriety. It looks like a driver's license photo courtesy of the DMV.

There's no photo of me but I am mentioned prominently, a little too prominently for my taste, as if this whole investigation was my idea. Maybe it's Lou Cioffi trying to butter me up. He wouldn't be the first newspaper reporter with a screenplay hidden away in a desk drawer. Califano is depicted as a hardworking bloodhound. The poet-for-hire, Jesse T. Humphreys, can't say enough good things about Virginia and her blossoming talent. Emily Dickinson should have gotten such a send-off. All in all it's a great job except for one thing. There is no arrest record of any kind on Alexander Farnsworth, not even a traffic ticket. Nonetheless a bevy of murder suspects has been exposed to the public. Now we wait.

It's nearly eleven o'clock. I have been sitting at my desk poring over the article for the past twenty minutes. I would have gotten to it sooner but Jack Warner called an impromptu meeting for nine-thirty to get a progress report on the Oscar situation. Charlie and I filled him in on everything that's being done and he called it a good start. Warner, who has a handle on the films being shot and whatever's in the pipeline, gave us his assessment of the competition.

Most of all he's pissed that the studio hasn't grabbed a Best Picture Oscar since 'Casablanca' seven years ago. In between, everybody's gotten a piece of the pie. RKO, Universal, Fox, Columbia, and Paramount twice. 'The Glass Menagerie' is going to change all that. Joe Mankiewicz thinks he has a lock with 'All About Eve'. He's dead wrong, Warner told us. Bette Davis will sink that picture's chances all by herself. 'Sunset Boulevard's the only real competition because you never underestimate Billy Wilder. What's left? Not much. Three comedies, 'Born Yesterday', "Harvey" and "Father of the Bride" No problem. Comedies never win. He scoffed at the likelihood of 'Cyrano' and 'King Solomon's Mines'. He's already got the Oscar on his mantlepiece.

As for the women, Gloria Swanson looks formidable, Davis has a chance if this is a year for scenery chewing by old has-beens. That leaves three spots which could conceivably be taken by three gals. Who else? Anne Baxter. No, she's supporting.

Judy Holliday? Comediennes don't win. Period. Deborah Kerr? Bloodless. Sexless. Don't be silly. No, the signs are all there. This is going to be a Warners year.

The thing I love about Jack Warner is, he's often wrong but he's never in doubt. This year, he may even be right.

The phone rings. Glenda Mae buzzes me.

"Ralph Twining. He says he's Lucretia Jenks' doctor," Glenda Mae tells me.

"I'll take it." I pick up the phone. "This is Joe Bernardi."

The man on the line has a confident patrician voice.

"Ralph Twining, Mr. Bernardi. I'm Lucretia Banks personal physician. I'm also her closest confidante. You may have seen me at the memorial service."

"I did. What can I do for you?" I ask.

"Mrs. Jenks would like to meet with you. Would noon today be convenient?"

"I can squeeze her in," I say.

"Excellent," he says. He sounds genuinely pleased. He gives me the address. I am momentarily concerned. My shabby Ford will be out of place. Maybe I should rent a limo for a couple of hours. Then I think, no, take me as I am or don't take me at all. I say I'll be there.

The house, if you can call it that, is on Roxbury on the flat-lands of Beverly Hills. It is situated on a lot big enough to handle my little Valley dwellng ten times over. The style is antebellum Alabama and the only thing missing are the slaves picking cot-ton in the front yard. The house to its left is a low lying Spanish hacienda which is owned by a matinee idol who hasn't had a decent picture in six years. I doubt he'll be a neighbor long. On the other side is a faux English Tudor which I believe is a winter home for a Minnesota beer baron whose net worth is measured in 8 figures and the first one is either a 5 or a 6. At the moment he seems not to be in residence although a crew of landscapers are busy mowing the lawn and tending to the bushes, trees and gardens. Beverly Hills, to the uninitiated, is a place where poverty is defined as a one story house on a one acre lot with only one car in the garage.

Dr. Twining's clinic on wheels is parked in the driveway and I pull in behind him. I do not park on the street. Cars not familiar to the local police have been known to disappear, towed away by the cops and never heard from again. Judge Roy Bean had nothing on the police chief of Beverly Hills.

I ring the door chime. A housekeeper admits me and Dr. Twining greets me in the foyer. I remember him from the service and in person he is just as patrician as his voice on the phone. We shake hands in greeting and he guides me to the staircase which leads to the second floor.

"Mrs. Jenks has been upset all morning," he tells me, "ever since she read the article in this morning's Times."

"I imagine she is. Is she well enough to talk?"

Twining smiles. "Oh, yes. No doubt you have heard that Lucretia is old and frail and has only weeks or months to live."

"I've heard rumors to that effect," I say.

"That's all they are, Mr. Bernardi, just rumors. Oh, she is not a really healthy woman, her inactivity has seen to that and her scoliosis is pronounced, but she is far from terminal, as much as her daughter and the boyfriend would like to believe."

I look at him, surprised.

He smiles again. "She likes to keep that information to herself. I cooperate. I hope you will, too."

"Absolutely," I say.

She is sitting up in a king sized canopy bed. Three pillows are behind her and a mahogany breakfast tray is sitting in her lap. It appears me to me she is lunching on a cheeseburger, french fried potatoes and a gibson martini. The LA Times is at her side, open to Cioffi's article. At the foot of the bed is a plump calico cat who is feasting from a sterling silver platter on what appears to be chunks of lobster or crab. A silk bib has been hung around its neck.

Lucretia Banks is a small woman, very thin with snow white hair and she is wearing thick lensed wire framed glasses. She looks up and peers at me over the frames.

"You are a troublesome man, Mr. Bernardi," she says in a voice that is strong but gravely.

"I try to be," I say. I look around for a chair. "May I sit?" I ask.

"I prefer that you don't," she says, "This won't take long." She picks up the newspaper in her claw-like fingers, looks at it momentarily, and then tosses it aside. "I assume," she continues, "that this is your handiwork."

I shrug in denial. "No, you have that wrong, Mrs.Jenks."

"Don't play me for a fool," she snaps. "I know exactly what you have been up to the past few days." She points at the paper. "This writer, this Mr. Cioffi, makes it clear that you are far from a disinterested observer. I realize you despised my daughter for trying to pass off your work as her own---"

"You are wrong, Mrs. Jenks---"

"Don't interrupt me, young man," she warns testily.

"I will interrupt you, madam, when you have no idea what you are talking about."

She is taken aback. "Excuse me."

"No, I will not excuse you. Initially, I was upset with Virginia but when I came to know the circumstances, I felt badly for her and actually came to like her a great deal. Her death is a tragedy and if possible I am going to find out who is responsible."

She stares at me thoughtfully and then drains the dregs of her gibson martini. She snaps her fingers at her doctor.

"Ralph, take this tray away and then bring over a chair for Mr. Bernardi." Twining hurries to her side and whisks away the tray. Lucretia looks over at the cat. "Muffin, come to mother." Without hesitation, the calico does as it's told and curls up in her mistresses' lap. Amazing. Say 'Come' to the average cat and it'll spit in your eye. What does the cat know that I don't?

Twining brings me a chair and I sit. Lucretia dismisses him from the room. He leaves without a whimper. I find myself growing ever more curious about the strange powers of this emaciated woman.

"You suspect my daughter Olivia of having poisoned Virginia."

"I suspect a lot of people," I say.

"But Olivia more than others."

I pause for a moment. "Top of my list," I say. "She and the boyfriend."

She smiles tightly. "Farnsworth," she says. "So cultured, so educated, so mannered----"

I finish it for her. "So full of crap."

"Precisely," she says. "Although I am forced to admit that, I may, and I emphasize the word 'may', may be wrong about him."

"In what way?" I ask.

"I was sure from the beginning that Alex Farnsworth's interest in Olivia had nothing to do with her limited charms and everything to do with my substantial fortune. No doubt the same thought has occurred to you, Mr. Bernardi."

"It has," I say.

"And if true, then Virginia's death may have been a way of

solidifying Olivia's claim to every dollar of my estate on my passing, which as you can imagine, might be tomorrow."

"Doubtful," I say.

She glares at me sourly and then continues. "And, of course, should that be true, then I myself might be in considerable danger so I took Olivia aside and laid out certain facts."

"Which are?"

"That she and her sister Virginia were not, and never had been, in line to inherit my money. Upon my passing, except for a few modest bequests to the household help, every dime will be passed on to Muffin."

I'm not sure I hear this right, I look at the cat, that big fat reddish-furred blob of inactivity.

"Your cat." I say.

"My cat," she replies. "The only person in the world who has consistently given me unstinting love and affection."

I am loath to remind her that Muffin is not a person. On the other hand, this revelation takes away the major motive for Olivia killing off Virginia. What would be the point?

"And when exactly did you make this known to your loving offspring?"

"Over a month ago," she says.

A month. Long before Virginia was murdered.

"So you see, Mr. Bernardi," Lucretia says, "if you are looking for a motive for one of my daughters killing the other, I think you will have to look elsewhere."

She's right, of course. And now I haven't a clue as to how to proceed. We chat for a minute or two longer and then I get up to leave. She's done with me and the feeling is mutual. As I head for the door, I turn back. She is gently stroking Muffin's fur and the cat looks content. So would I with that much money coming my way.

"A word of advice, Mrs. Jenks," I say. "Now that the cat's out of the bag, no pun intended, I would think seriously about about a bodyguard for dear little Muffin. Very seriously."

Lucretia smiles at me. "For obvious reasons, Mr. Bernardi, I no longer permit Olivia or Mr. Farnsworth into my house."

I smile back. I try to picture Farnsworth being thwarted by a door lock or intimidated by a bedridden old woman. That cat had better have nine lives. More, if possible.

Twining is waiting for me and walks me to the door. I tell him that I found Mrs. Jenks to be feisty and far from sickly but I express concern about her mental state.

He smiles. "You mean the will?"

"I do," I say. "The kittycat may think its coming into a pile of dough but me, I see a platoon of lawyers in its future."

"Not so, Mr. Bernardi. We've had the provisions analyzed by experts. It is uncontestable."

"I see," I say. "Out of curiosity, when the inevitable occurs, who becomes guardian of the cat?"

Twining smiles again. "That responsibility falls to me, Mr. Bernardi. I plan to execute my duties most diligently."

I smile back at him. I'll bet he does.

I head back to the office but I no sooner walk in the door than Glenda Mae stops me. "Oswald Pennybaker. He says it's urgent."

"Get him for me."

When he comes on the phone, I say, "Nice article."

"Everything we hoped for," Oswald says. "And it's starting to pay off."

"What's up?"

"Come on over," he says. "It's worth the drive."

By now I know Oswald well enough to know he won't waste

my time with something trivial or irrelevant. It is nearly two o'clock and I am slightly annoyed. I haven't eaten and when I don't eat I get cranky. Nonetheless, I hop in my car and drive over to The Garden of Allah. The sky is greyish and when I get out of my car I realize the place looks even worse than it did the other day. It won't be long before the hookers and the dopers take over.

Oswald's standing on his stoop smoking a cigarette and looking across the way at Virginia's unit. I notice that her door is open.

"I thought the cops were through with her place," I say.

"They are," Oswald says.

Just then Maybelle Ruskin emerges from the doorway carrying a cardboard carton which she places on the walkway. She looks up and sees me, smiles and waves and then goes back inside.

"She's not wasting any time, is she?" I say.

"Not so's I noticed," Oswald says as we go up the walkway and into the bungalow.

"Good morning," Maybelle says looking up from a pile of old magazines which she is leafing through. She's wearing a faded pair of oversized slacks and a baggy sweater and she's tied a bandana around her head. Satisfied there's nothing in the pile, she tosses them into a large trash barrel that sits in the middle of the room.

"Good morning to you, Miss Ruskin," I say. "Need some help?"

She shakes her head. "Doing just fine, thanks," she says.

"Guess you saw this morning's Times."

"I did. Glad to see somebody's finally paying attention to poor Virginia's death." She turns her attention to a nearby cardboard carton and hefts it up onto the table.

"She must have loved you very much," I say, "leaving you everything the way she did."

"Well, I'm grateful, of course, but I think I got everything mainly out of a process of elimination." She pops open the carton and starts to sift through it's contents.

Oswald had wandered off into the kitchen and now he returns carrying a glass of water. "Looking for anything in particular, Miss Ruskin?" he asks.

"Poems," she says. "Virginia wrote all the time. What she showed me was only a fraction of her work. The rest has to be around here somewhere."

"Figuring on printing some of it?" Oswald asks.

"You're damned right. You read what Jesse T. Humphreys said about Virginia's talent. A new and vibrant Amy Lowell. More prescient than Gertrude Stein. A lively heiress to the mantle of Anne Bronte. With that kind of publicity a new volume of Virginia's work will be an overnight best seller."

"Maybe she didn't show you the other stuff because it isn't any good," I suggest.

"Unimportant and irrelevant. If Lizzie Borden had written a novel she'd have outsold Mark Twain. Notoriety, that's what sells, Mr. Bernardi." She laughs. "That's funny. Me telling you, a movie publicist, how the public can be boondoggled."

I smile. "Yes, ma'am, that is funny."

"Then again," Oswald says, "if the new book doesn't sell, you can always fall back on that thirty five thousand dollar insurance payoff."

Maybelle throws him a dirty look. "I hope you're not hinting at what I think you're hinting at, old timer."

"Merely an observation," he says.

"Because if you are, you're spitting in the wrong spitoon. I loved that girl, yes I did, and I would never have hurt her in any way. I know you have to think like a cop because that's who you are but I promise you this, you make any kind of accusation like that in public, you'd better be able to back it up."

Oswald nods. "Should the occasion arise, believe me, I will be prepared."

She stares at him hard and then looks over at me. "Thanks for dropping by," she says. "The door's over there."

She waits. We get the hint. We leave. As we go she opens another box scouring for poems by the new and vibrant heir to Amy Lowell's mantle.

When I get back to the studio, all hell has been broken loose. Charlotte Schroeder has left a message and I return her call. She is beside herself. Why has her picture appeared in the paper? Why has she been lumped together with those other people as if she were a murder suspect? I loved Virginia, she says so adamantly you almost believe her. Emma Schroeder has also called. Emma, who has gotten the wrong end of the stick every time she's turned around, is just plain pissed and needs someone to scream at besides her boyfriend Assistant District Attorney Harlow Quinn. And then there's Charlie who has heard from Jack Warner who has heard from Quinn. Quinn roasted me up and down to Warner who called Charlie demanding to know what was going on and Charlie called me, warning me that I may have gotten my name in the paper one time too many. Warner is quick to flare and most of the time just as quick to forget. Charlie tells me to pray that this is one of those times.

The call comes in just after five o'clock. I'd let Glenda Mae go early for a dentist appointment so I answer the phone myself. As I do I think to myself, this is the third call of the day. Is it good things that come in threes or is it bad? I can't remember.

"Bernardi."

"Joseph Bernardi?" a man asks. He's speaking quietly, not quite a whisper but definitely muffled.

"That's right."

"I read the story in the newspaper," he says.

"Okay."

"I didn't know the young lady. I liked what I read about her."

"I didn't catch your name, sir," I say.

"My name is not important," he says. "I have information for you."

"What kind of information?" I ask.

"About the art gallery. There are problems over there. Major problems."

"I know. They're going broke."

"That, too," he says.

"What do you mean, that, too?"

"No, not on the phone. We have to meet."

"Where? When?"

"Tonight. I think I'm being watched."

"By who? What for?"

"There's a restaurant near the corner of Wilshire and Western. Skipper Sam's. They close at ten but after nine they're pretty empty. I'll meet you there at nine o'clock."

"How will I know you?"

"I'll be sitting in the farthest booth to the left when you walk in the door. I'll have a briefcase on the floor next to me."

"Can you give me some idea---"

"Nine o'clock.Come alone. What I have is for your eyes only. If you're not there by ten after, I leave." And he hangs up.

I'm not sure I like the sound of this but I wanted to get involved and now I'm involved. Besides, what can happen in a public place? I am intrigued by his reply, "That, too." I can't wait to find out what that's all about.

I call Bunny at the house hoping she's already gotten home and she has. We had planned a hamburger and movie date tonight and I apologize for having to beg off. When she finds out why, she is very leery.

"What is all this, Joe? Skipper Sam's? Sounds like a bad movie. Why doesn't he just come to your office?"

"I don't know. Maybe he's shy."

"I think it stinks. Don't go," she says. "If he calls again, tell him you'll meet him in broad daylight in the Rose Bowl parking lot."

"Bunny, I love you but you worry too much. This may break open the case. I've got no choice."

"Have you forgotten there's a killer running around loose?"

"Stop worrying. Fix yourself a bite to eat, grab a beer and curl up on the couch with Uncle Miltie. I'll be home by eleven. Scout's honor." I make a kissing sound and hang up. The last thing I need is more hand wringing from Bunny. I'm perfectly capable of taking care of myself.

On the other hand....

I grab a burger and a coke to go at Bob's Big Boy and drive over to Beverly Hills where I park on Rodeo Drive directly across the street from Le Chalet d'Arte. The front is mostly window, better to show off the masterpieces within and I can see Olivia and Alex hobnobbing with a half dozen customers. They're imbibing champagne and it's all laughs and smiles and God knows what else but I assume for the gallery, that's business as usual. I eat the burger, drink the coke and keep watching. The hulk appears. He joins the merriment. I see a lot of drinking. I don't see much buying. By eight-thirty I am convinced that Alex is going to stay put for the evening. I start the car and drive off to the corner of Wilshire and Western.

It takes me two drive-bys to find it because Skipper Sam's is between two larger buildings and set back from the street. There's a small eight car parking lot in front and low level lighting coming from inside. This is called ambience. And my caller wasn't kidding about business being slow after nine p.m. The place looks deserted.

I get out of my car and walk to the entrance. There's a sign in the doorway. Breakfast 7-11. Lunch 11-3. Closed for Dinner. I peer in through the glass door. What I mistook for ambience are low wattage night lights. I am suddenly caught in approaching headlights as a car pulls into the small parking lot and stops sideways behind my car so that I can't back out. The car's headlights extinguish and the doors open. Three men get out and start to walk toward me. One of them is holding a baseball bat.

CHAPTER EIGHTEEN

I've never been introduced to the guy with the baseball bat and frankly, I don't want to be. He's short, maybe five-six, but with muscles that threaten to cause tears in his tight fitting pants and tee shirt. He's totally bald and has no eyebrows that I can see. His lips are full and fat and seem to form a perpetual sneer. His nose seems to have been broken more times than a gigolo's promises. He reminds me a little of Jackie Coogan but not as handsome. When he speaks his voice reminds me of Jane Withers.

"I think you have a problem," he says.

"I do," I say. "Many. Which one are we talking about?" Externally I am jocular but I can't take my eyes off that damned bat.

"You need to learn to mind your own business."

"I try but it's difficult. I'm just naturally nosy. A failing."

"You talk to cops. Also a failing."

He holds out the bat, flips it and catches it on the barrel end, then takes a vicious swipe at my leg with the handle. Pain shoots up my entire body and I gasp, momentarily unable to breathe.

"Do you have anything funny to say about that?" he asks.

"Not off hand," I croak, reaching down and rubbing my leg vigorously. Ballplayers say you shouldn't rub your aches. I'm not a ballplayer.

"I could have broken your leg if I had used the other end of the bat," he says. "If I'd swung at your head, I could have killed you. I'm not going to kill you. Not this time."

"Nice of you," I say.

He swings hard at my arm, hitting the muscle between my shoulder and my elbow. Again the pain tears at me.

Baldy shakes his head. "You just can't keep your mouth shut, can you?" he says. He swings again, this time the other leg and I go down on my knees, dizzy. He moves closer standing over me.

"Listen good, friend," he says. "Next time I'll turn the bat around and use it on your head. You understand?" I nod. "Good. You tell that newspaper guy Cioffi, he'd better back off or he gets it, too. You tell him that." He waits for me to respond. "You hear me?"

"Yes, I hear you."

Just then lights flood the parking area as an unmarked van wails into the parking lot and screeches to a halt. We all turn to look as a man jumps out of the driver's side holding a pump action shotgun. A second man emerges from the passenger side. He, too, is armed. One look and Baldy's cohorts take off running.

"Hold it!" the man yells pumping a shell into the chamber. The two goons are not about to halt for anybody. Baldy turns and he, too, starts to run. The man fires into the air and pumps again. "Freeze, asshole, or I put one in your back!"

Baldy freezes in place, lifting his hands. "On the ground and spread 'em," the newcomer orders. Baldy does as he's told.

"Cuff him, Don", the man says to his partner, "then radio the cops." The man approaches me, shaking his head. I thought I'd recognized his voice. Now I see who it is. Mick Clausen is a successful bail bondsman who is married to my ex-wife Lydia and is also a good friend.

"Are you okay?" he asks.

"A little pain here and there," I manage to say. "What are you doing here?"

"Your lady love called and said you weren't allowed out after dark without a chaperone. I volunteered."

"Thanks."

"No problem. Lydia would have my head if I let anything happen to you. She still likes you. Can't think why."

I'm about to say something witty when the pain grabs me again and I gasp. Mick reacts. "Bad?" he asks.

"Bad enough," I say.

Mick turns and yells over to the van. "Don, tell the cops we'll meet them at Mount Sinai Hospital!" He turns to me. "Can you walk?"

"I think so," I say, struggling to my feet. The pain is all over but it's not debilitating. I think kind thoughts about a doctor who may shortly give me a shot of something or at the very least some very helpful pills.

Mick helps me toward the van letting me lean on him. His associate Don gets out of the car and approaches. Mick tosses him the gun and nods toward Baldy who is lying on the pavement, hands cuffed behind his back. "Toss that sack of shit on the backseat and if he looks at you cross-eyed, blow his fucking head off."

Forty-five minutes later I'm sitting on an examination bed in Mount Sinai's emergency ward. A doctor has examined me carefully and assured me I have no broken bones. By tomorrow I will be sporting some ugly looking purple and yellow bruises but they will fade with time. He has been kind enough to jab me in the butt with a hypo full of demerol and I am already feeling its effects. I start whistling 'If I Knew You Were Coming I'd Have Baked a Cake." Mick regards me with amusement.

At that moment Sergeant Aaron Kleinschmidt enters.

"Who belongs to that piece of human garbage cuffed to the door handle of the van out there?" he asks.

Mick raises his hand.

Kleinschmidt nods. "It figures." He looks over at me. "And you? When are you going to stop getting your name plastered all over the metro radio system?"

"Working on it," I say.

"So what is it this time, Joe?" he asks.

I tell him. He listens intently and when I am finished, he asks, "And you have no idea who sent him?"

"Oh, I have an idea," I say, "but nothing I could prove."

"Alexaner Farnsworth?" Kleinschmidt asks. He is familiar with the Jenks murder case.

"Who else?" I respond.

"I assume you're going to press charges," Kleinschmidt says.

"Absolutely," I say, "and I want you to squeeze this guy until he'd give up his mother for bottle feeding him."

Kleinschmidt nods. "He'll get my total attention." He turns to Mick. "Can you get him home, Mick?"

Mick nods. "Don and I can handle it."

"Okay. I'll have the uniforms book your baboon into Metro and I'll take a run at him. If I get anything I'll let you know."

"Thanks, Aaron," Mick says.

Kleinschmidt nods and looks over at me, pointing a finger. "And you, stop trying to be a goddamned hero all the time. You're thirty years old, out of shape and you couldn't fight your way out of a kindergarten free-for-all."

"Point taken," I say, wondering if the doctor is going to give me some pills to take home with me. As it turns out, he does.

Mick and Don take me back to the restaurant to pick up my

car which Mick drives to my house. When I get home and walk through the door, I expect Bunny to throw her arms around me in relief that I am well and unharmed. Instead she throws her arms around Mick and holds him tight in gratitude for his saving my life. I think the hug is a little too tight and it lasts a little too long but maybe that's just the demerol working.

With Mick's help, Bunny gets me in the bedroom where they strip me down, put me under the covers and leave the room, turning out the lights. I pray that sleep will come quickly. Before I can give it a second thought I am snoring peacefully.

The next morning I arrive at the office about a half hour late and aching all over. I didn't take my pills with breakfast because I had to drive but now, in my office, I down four of them with my morning coffee. Glenda Mae, who cannot see my bruises and whom I keep in the dark about my stupidity the previous evening, thinks I am behaving like a doofus. This is because the first thing she told me when I walked in the door was that Charlie Berger wanted to see me. Now with the pills in my system, I ask her what's new. She looks at me funny. Charlie Berger. His office. Now.

Charlie is not in a good mood and he wastes no time in getting to the point. "I don't know how but somehow J.L. found out about your little adventure last night and to put it bluntly, he is no longer amused. Effective immediately, you are suspended without pay for a period of two weeks."

"Oh, now wait, Charlie---"

"And don't whine about it. The suspension is my idea. J.L. wanted to fire you."

"But----"

"There are no buts, Joe. Go back to your office, clear up any loose ends, and go home. And also have your secretary forward all your phone calls to this office, effective immediately."

"Charlie, I---"

"Is that clear, Joe? Say yes and get out of here."

I stare at him for a moment, then throw up my hands in disgust and walk out. I can find things to do at home. Maybe I'll put up the screens. Maybe I'll weed the garden. Maybe I'll start another novel.

I'm back at my office rummaging through my desk drawers, looking for stuff to steal to replenish my supplies at home, things like rubber bands and paper clips. I've already told Glenda Mae to forward my calls to Charlie. I look at my desk stapler. The one I had at home broke. I regard it enviously, debating whether I should "borrow" it.

"Hey!" I look up. Sergeant Kleinschmidt is standing in the doorway.

"Good morning, Sarge," I say.

"Your lady said I could walk right in."

"That's because you're on the A-list."

"What's the A stand for?" he asks.

"You really don't want to know," I tell him.

"Is this a bad time or can I get a cup of coffee?"

"Help yourself," I tell him.

He disappears into Glenda Mae's domain and returns a few moments later with a mug of joe. He sits down. The phone rings. I'm about to tell Glenda Mae to hold all calls when I remember that they are being forwarded to Charlie and I'm not supposed to be here.

"I spent a couple of fruitful hours last night chatting with Joe DiMaggio," Kleinschmidt says.

"Tell me," I say, leaning back in my desk chair.

"His name is Hollister Dunn. This I was able to get off of his Louisiana driver's license. We've got nothing in our system so on a hunch, first thing this morning, I called the New Orleans police department. Bingo. Hollister, or Hockie as he is known to the NOPD, has a rap sheet as long as Pinocchio's nose. He is into everything with the emphasis on strong arm. Assault, extortion, and other forms of bodily mayhem. I ask about associates. I'm told he is and has been very close to a wheeler dealer named Gilbert Cass. Cass is your typical con man, charming, good looking, smooth talking ---"

"And probably looks a lot like Alexander Farnsworth." The phone rings again. What's going on? I'm really not that popular.

"Indeed he does," Kleinschmidt says. "And you know what this bozo's speciality is? Art fraud. Promoting it, selling it and even making it. He has a guy working for him that can create Vermeers on demand."

"Now let me guess. He uses his social skills to worm his way into a legitimate operation and then starts unloading his fakes onto an unsuspecting public."

"And who more unsuspecting than overpaid, not so bright Hollywood types?" Kleinschmidt says. "Now since there are a couple of Louisiana warrants out on Hockie as well as this Gil Cass, I hint around that maybe, if he is cooperative enough, no charges will be filed and he will be free to go. Hockie starts singing like Sinatra at the Paramount."

"If you got anything worthwhile, I'm amenable." Now yet another phone call. I'm starting to get curious about this sudden activity.

"Thought you would be," Kleinschmidt says. "Here's the good stuff. Gil Cass has a record. Did a year in state prison on a fraud beef when he was real young. Since then he's smartened up. Hockie also says he's married and maybe to more than one woman. Marries 'em, uses 'em and disappears."

"This should be of great interest to Olivia Jenks."

"I agree. Now here's the bad part. He breathes larceny but when it comes to violence, he begs off. Partly because it's the way he is, partly common sense. Violence can get you a lot of years in the penitentiary or worse, a visit to the chair."

"You believe him?"

"It makes sense, Joe. Con men are cowards at heart. They almost never get involved in rough stuff."

"So what are you saying, Sarge?" I ask. "Farnsworth nee Cass will rob you blind but he hasn't got the balls or the inclination to hurt you?"

"That sums it up," Kleinschmidt says.

"Even a hands-off, remote killing like the one that did in Virginia?"

"I don't know. He's got the perfect motive and a huge amount of money's involved. I guess it's possible. I just don't think so."

"You going to move on him for the art fraud?"

Kleinschmidt nods. "We've lined up an out of town appraiser. Soon as we get a warrant we're going to take the place down and see what we find."

"I'd love to be there," I say hopefully.

Kleinschmidt gets up from his chair smiling. "We'll see," he says. He goes to the door and turns. "By the way. The coffee. Terrific. Chickory, right?"

I nod. "Chickory, right."

"Thought so." He winks and leaves.

I lean back in my chair and I'm torn. In my mind I already had Olivia and/or Alex doing twenty to life for killing Virginia. God knows they have ample motive and in Alex's case, a total lack of scruples. But Kleinschmidt says probably not and he's a sharp cop. I don't think he's wrong very often. Now what?

Glenda Mae buzzes me. Mr. Berger wants to see me in his office immediately. More trouble. I walk down the corridor expecting the worst. Maybe Warner really does want me out of here. Maybe I'm out of a job.

Charlie looks at me across his desk. There's a lined yellow pad in front of him and then he glances at it and then back at me.

"I forgot we have that kitchen photo shoot wth Eleanor this Friday."

"Everything's arranged," I say. "Piece of cake."

"She was not thrilled to hear that you won't be there."

"She gets nervous. She'll be fine."

He looks at his pad again.

"Did you know that Jane Wyman is wandering all over New Orleans looking for Tennessee Williams? Something about a joint interview."

"We discussed it informally. Nothing in concrete," I say.

"That's not what she thinks," Charlie says sourly. "And who the hell is Fanny Holtzman?"

"I think she's Gertrude Lawrence's manager."

"Swell," Charlie says. "Were you aware that Miss Lawrence wants us to send a Pathe newsreel crew to Aruba tomorrow afternoon to film a tete a tete between her and Noel Coward about her upcoming role in 'The Glass Menagerie'?"

"We never got into that," I say.

"Well, that's what she wants," he growls. "Aruba, Jesus Christ," he mutters. "And oh, yeah, after that she's flying into New York for a very important meeting and also to do this new television show that's on CBS Thursday night." He peers down at the pad. "What's My Line? What the hell is What's My Line?"

Charlie rips the lined yellow sheet from the pad and hands it to me. "Here. Take care of this."

"I'm on suspension," I remind him.

"Well, if you think I'm going to deal with these three babes, you're out of your mind. Suspension suspended. Get to work."

I smile. "You're the boss."

As I stride down the hallway back to my office, I'm amazed at Gertrude Lawrence's self-serving chutzpah as if I didn't know my job. I'm also wondering how quickly I can get a camera crew into Aruba.

CHAPTER NINETEEN

That evening, Bunny and I have our date, twenty four hours late. At six-thirty we're sitting in a booth at the Beef and Beans Diner which, a couple of years ago, was called The Egg and I. My friend Phil tried to make a living out of a place that sold only omelets and was basically open only for breakfast and brunch. As he was about to go under he wised up, changed the name, changed the menu and switched to a 24 hour a day schedule. Whereas he had once prided himself in offering 56 different kinds of omelets, now he promotes 56 different types of burgers, about half of which are edible. The same can be said for his 21 different side orders of beans.

I settle for a deadly dull All American burger which even Phil cannot screw up and a side of Boston baked. Bunny, braver than me by far, opts for the Delhi Delight, a half pound patty smothered with porcini mushrooms, artichoke leaves and a highly spiced Indian curry. For a side she chooses garbanzo beans in tomato aspic.

We laugh a lot, especially when I tell her about Muffin, the millionaire cat, who dines on lobster. She is not surprised to learn about Farnsworth's actual persona. She had him spotted as a phony from the first. She professes to be a little sorry for him.

She hears the Louisiana chain gangs can be particularly oppressive in the summer months which are right around the corner. Neither of us mentions the 800 pound gorilla which is sitting on our table between the salt and pepper and the paper napkin dispenser. I fight the urge to ask if Walt has called her. Bad news travels fast. I don't want to egg it on.

The simple truth is, I'm terrified. I am thirty years old and I have never loved or been loved more than in my relationship with Bunny. I thought I'd found it with Lydia but I know now that our marriage was a fraud, something born out of wartime angst. I was twenty-three and headed for Europe. She was twenty and in love with the idea of love. We never had a chance and when I came back at war's end, it was more pride than love that made me try to salvage our relationship. Love has always eluded me from the time I was born to a woman who gave me up before I was a month old. Foster mothers have no time for love, they are too busy meting out discipline and trying to keep order. I think of Walt. Not Bunny's Walt, my Walt. The hero of my book. Like Walt I ran away from a foster home when I was fifteen and caught on in the Texas oil fields. And like Walt I fell in love with the owner's daughter who was a worldly wise twenty one. I didn't get her pregnant and I didn't kill anybody but I did get the crap beaten out of me and I did run for my life the first chance I got. I learned later that she told her Daddy that I had seduced her when it was the other way around. No wonder that I started dealing with women with great caution. No wonder that I was building a protective wall all about me. Until Lydia I did not get hurt again but I paid for it with days and nights of loneliness. I look across the table at Bunny and she is smiling and prattling on about something funny that happened at the office but I am only half listening. Have I found this wonderful woman who has opened up my world only to lose her? I know I must stop dwelling on it. I have no control. What will be will be but I am sick at heart.

At eight o'clock we hit the neighborhood theater to catch "The Asphalt Jungle" which has just opened. It is the best Warner Brothers movie that Warners didn't produce. It's a heist picture directed by good friend, John Huston, and though it is full of B elements, it is taut and fast moving and features a terrific performance by Sterling Hayden. There's also this blonde newcomer with a bit part whose name I'm not sure of but it is spelled s-e-x-k-i-t-t-e-n. Margery Monroe. Something like that. She may have a future.

When we get home it's ten thirty and both of us are ready for sleep. The phone rings. I look at Bunny. She looks at me. I wave my finger at it as if to say, your call. She goes to it and lifts the receiver, expecting it to be Walt Davenport. After a moment she hands it to me. I think she's disappointed but it's hard to tell. I take it. It's Kleinschmidt. He has good news for me.

The next morning I am standing next to the painting of the guy in the jock strop holding the cat. It's shortly after eleven. A dozen or more people, some in uniform, are milling about. Kleinschmidt, armed with a search warrant, has seized the company books. He also has a fugitive warrant in his pocket for Gilbert Cass, aka Alex Farnsworth, but is waiting to serve it until most of the search and seizure work has been finished. Lou Cioffi is here. So is Daniel David Doyle, the art critic. He's not expert enough to tell if either the Lautrec or the Hals are fakes but if they are, they are awfully good ones, he tells me. The out-of-state appraiser has already made his cursory examination but he won't be able to state anything with certainty until he has subjected the paintings to a series of scientific tests. I have no doubt what his verdict will be.

Olivia Jenks is off in a corner, away from the hubbub. She has been crying. Doyle is with her offering sympathy and a shoulder to cry on. Twice Farnsworth has tried to talk to her and twice she has loudly told him to leave her alone. Either she is a terrific actress or she had no idea what her lover boy was up to. I tend to believe the latter. Those tears are genuine.

Cioffi has already talked to the appraiser and now he's in deep conversation with Aaron Kleinschmidt. Lou's got another big story for tomorrow's edition though I'm not sure this gets us any closer to answering the big question.

Farnsworth is standing solemnly by the front window staring out at the passersby on Rodeo Drive. No one's coming in because a uniformed cop is stationed by the doorway to turn away gawkers.

I walk over thinking I will engage him in a friendly chat.

"Guess you're sorry now that your boy didn't kill me when he had the chance," I say. It seems like a nice ice-breaker. Farnsworth looks at me coldly. "Probably even more sorry Hockie didn't get away like the other two. You wouldn't be in this mess."

"You're amused. Go ahead. Enjoy it," he says. "This whole thing is a huge misunderstanding."

"No doubt," I say. "Although you do have a certain reputation."

"I do," he says, "and it is one of honesty and integrity."

"Really?" I say with amusement. "That's not how they feel down in New Orleans." I pronounce it like one word: Nawleans.

Farnsworth looks at me sharply. Oops, he must be thinking, this guy knows something but what and how much? "New Orleans? What's New Orleans got to do with me?" he complains.

"Actually, a great deal, Gil." I hit that 'Gil' hard and again he reacts.

"What the hell are you talking about?" he says in annoyance.

Good. He's going to try to bluff it out.

"The only thing the cops don't have, Gil, is the name of your artiste," I say. "Long on talent, short on originality. Is he here with you in Los Angeles or did you leave him back in the bayous?"

He starts to walk away. "Go bother somebody else," he says.

"Suit yourself," I say. "I just thought I might be able to help you out with the cops."

He turns back. "Yeah? And how do you figure on doing that?"

"Look, I don't give a rat's rear end about your con game or your phony paintings. I want to know who killed Virginia and while I'm pretty sure it wasn't you, maybe you know something that'll point me in the right direction."

"I don't," he says.

"Maybe you think you don't. Tell me about Virginia."

"There's nothing to tell. I never met her."

"Really?"

"Yes, really, Mr. Bernardi. I met Olivia last August. At that time, she had not spoken to Virginia in over a year."

"Then you never met Leon."

He smiles. "Actually, I did. It was right after New Year's. I gave him a call. I wanted to find out what his game was. You see, in my line of work you believe that everybody has a game. He invited me to the bungalow at The Garden of Allah on a day when Virginia was attending a poetry seminar."

"So you were actually in the bungalow," I say.

"I just said that. What's your point?"

"Nothing. Go on."

"It didn't take me long to figure out that he had no game, at least not my kind of game. He was just this poor schlub who was convinced he had written the so-called great American novel and it was going to make him rich."

I smile inwardly. This was starting to get interesting.

"You say poor schlub. How so?"

He shakes his head at my apparent denseness. "Come on, fella. He had mama's boy written all over him. Oh, sure, I guess you could describe him as caring and sensitive and gentle. Not me. He had apron strings hanging all over him. Hey, if he thought some book was going to make him rich, more power to him but as far as old lady Jenks's estate went, he had no agenda and he was no threat. I got out of there as fast as I could."

I nod thoughtfully. "Did you use the bathroom?"

"What?"

"Did you go into the bathroom?"

"What the hell kind of a question is that?"

"Did you?"

"No, I didn't."

"And you didn't tamper with a medicine bottle?"

"Hell, no."

"Even though Virginia's death would make Olivia twice as rich?"

"The only one getting rich is that damned cat," he says.

"But you didn't know that at the time, did you?"

He glares at me. "You know something, Bernardi. I think you ask too many questions about things that are none of your business." He stalks past me. I watch him go. He's arrogant and surly and a thief right down to his core but I'm pretty sure he's too self-protective to commit murder. I wish I didn't feel that way. I need a viable suspect badly.

I head back to the studio, my head still filled with unanswered questions. For the tenth time I try to postulate suicide. I try to picture Virginia taking a medicine capsule, dumping the contents and substituting cyanide, all of this after I have just left her relieved and content and actually smiling. Or had she doctored the pill earlier and was holding it in abeyance. And if so why take it then? And why walk into the living room where she will fall over striking her head instead of sitting in a chair or going into the bedroom. No matter how I look at it, suicide is absurd.

Totally frustrated, I turn in the car radio. I could use a little music to distract me.

"...massing along the 38th parallel by the tens of thousands, a clear threat to the stability of the region. A nighttime sortie by North Korean forces succeeded in destroying an ammunition dump several kilometers south of the demilitarized zone. President Truman has called for an immediate meeting of members of the United Nations Security Council to deal with this act of aggression. South Korean president Syngman Rhee has asked for United Nations intervention including military forces to deal with this latest incursion..."

I flip off the radio. I don't want to hear any more. If the world has once again gone mad, I want no part of it. American blood was spilled all over Europe and on the islands and atolls of the South Pacific. I say, no more. I don't know where Korea is and more than that, I don't care. If the earth is once more going to spin out of control, it can do so without my participation.

I arrive at the studio, park and head for my office. I wave to a couple of people I know. They wave back. The lot is bustling with activity. If anyone is worried about a possible third world war, they don't show it.

Glenda Mae says I have had one call. Barry Loeb, my agent.

I call him back. He's checking in for a progress report on the book. I tell him Henry Blanke has it and he's enthused. Barry is pleased but he has to cut our conversation short. Orson Welles is on his other line.

I sit back in my chair. Tomorrow, Eleanor Parker's kitchen. Today, nothing. Jane Wyman? Silence. Gertrude Lawrence? Not a peep. The silence is soothing. I'd love to go home and take a nice long nap but it's only twelve-thirty. I get up from my desk and head out. I may stop by the commissary for lunch but first I stop by Henry Blanke's office. I pop my head in and smile at Vera, Henry's secretary.

'He's not here," she says. "He's scouting locations in San Diego."

"Okay. Just wanted to say hello," I say with a smile.

She nods knowingly. "It's still on the pile on his desk," she says. "There are three new scripts on top of it."

I manage another smile and thank her. I have just lost my appetite so I head back to my office. I sit down behind my desk. With a sigh I reach into the center drawer and take out a sheet of paper. I slip it into the typewriter and start to write.

EXCLUSIVE TO YOU IN YOUR AREA

CHAPTER TWENTY

Bored to tears I left work early and went home. Bunny will be along in an hour or so. I've stopped for dinner fixings at the market and I start by washing off some fresh romaine lettuce. I cut up a small boneless chicken breast into chunks and start to saute them in an aluminum fry pan. I toss a couple of russet potatoes into the oven at 400. They'll need about an hour. When they're just about ready, I'll chop up the lettuce, add the cooked chicken pieces and some store bought croutons, toss with a store bought caesar dressing, lay out a french baguette and some butter and voila, a meal fit for royalty. I love preparing this meal because it is foolproof. There is absolutely no way of screwing it up.

Bunny walks in a little after six. There's no bounce to her step and I can tell immediately something is wrong. I go to her and fold her into my arms. She clutches at me tightly for the longest time and then relaxes. Finally she lets go.

"I need a beer," she says.

"Bad news?"

"Define bad," she says.

I've pulled two beers from the fridge and uncapped them. I hand Bunny one. We both drink. She's put away half the bottle before she comes up for air.

"I heard from Walt," she says. "I won't be going to New York any time soon."

"Sorry," I say.

"Don't be. I was never sure I wanted to go but I was flattered that I was good enough to be asked. That's high praise for a little old corn-fed Nebraska farm girl."

I throw a mock glare in her direction. "Hey, this is me, remember? You haven't been in Nebraska since you were two years old, you hate corn and downtown Omaha ain't no farm."

"I was dramatizing for effect," she says. "Anyway, there were extenuating circumstances."

"Such as?"

"He said he can't afford to hire me because he needs a war correspondent. He says we're going to war, Joe. No question."

I shake my head. "Damn," I mutter under my breath.

Bunny smiles at me. "So no job for Bunny but he did say he'd hire you in a flash if you want the job."

"Me?"

"Probably had something to do with me describing you as the best damned war correspondent to come out of WWII."

"Oh, thanks, sweetheart. If he should happen to call again, tell him I have other wars to deal with right here at home."

She nods, then wrinkles up her nose. "Are you cooking something?"

I sniff the air. Uh oh. The damned potatoes. I hurry into the kitchen and open the oven door. They are black and smell like charcoal. So much for a dinner that only a moron could screw up.

Bunny and I make do with the chicken caesar and the baguette and a couple of beers and at eight o'clock we sit down in front of the television set to watch 'What's My Line?' Bunny asks why we are doing this and I tell her that Gertrude Lawrence is going to make an appearance. This will be excellent publicity for the film. Gertrude's a real pro when it comes to promoting herself and the projects she's in.

But when the program starts, Gertrude is nowhere to be seen. The show is one of those panel gabfests with an amiable man named John Daly as the moderator. On the panel are Arlene Francis, an actress with a modest career behind her, Broadway columnist Dorothy Kilgallen, a writer named Louis Untermeyer and a guy named Hal Block. As entertainment it's about as dumb as they come. A guest comes on and asking 'yes' or 'no' questions, the panel has to figure out what the guest does for a living. The first guy turns out to be a rodeo clown. A white haired Granny-type is next. She's the sheriff of a small town in Wyoming. Thankfully they go to commercial and I can't believe I'm watching this. If it lasts out the year I will be shocked. I look at Bunny. She's smiling. What a terrific idea for a show, she says. I love it, she says. I can only assume she's drunk.

It gets worse. They come back from commercial and now the panelists are all wearing masks. It's time for the celebrity guest. They cut to a blackboard and as the audience breaks into applause, a female hand places her autograph on the slate. Gertrude Lawrence.

I get suddenly excited. I realize that no one in his right mind could possibly be watching this program but any publicity is good publicity so I sit back to enjoy. Gertrude looks wonderful and she's having fun putting on a low pitched voice with a Transylvanian accent to disguise her voice. Just when it looks as if the panel is about to post another bagel, Francis asks three cogent questions in a row and identifies her. Much hilarity as masks come off and John Daly asks just the right question. "So, Miss Lawrence, what are you up to these days?"

I look at Bunny with a grin. These are the moments we publicists look forward to: national exposure free of charge and requiring minimal effort to pull off.

"Well, John," she says, "I have just spent most of the day chatting with two delightful gentlemen I'm sure all of us here know, Dick Rodgers and Oscar Hammerstein, who are writing a musical for me to star in next season on Broadway."

Huh? Musical? Next season? Hey, lady, what about our movie?

"It's called 'The King and I' and it's based on the memoirs of Anna Leonowens. Well, if you saw the film 'Anna and the King of Siam' you'll know who I'm talking about."

Much ooohing and ahhing among the panel members.

"I believe they are going after Rex Harrison to play the King but we're not sure he's available. Dick played a couple of the melodies for me and I'm sure it's going to be a wonderful experience."

The Glass Menagerie, I am screaming to myself to no avail. I hear Daly thank Gertrude for dropping by and she walks over to the panel to shake everyone's hand and then she is gone. I am sick. This musical has become all consuming to her. Our movie is an afterthought. Hardly worth mentioning which is exactly what happened.

Bunny tries to put a good face on it. "Maybe she forgot."

I arch an eyebrow in disbelief. "We are paying her tens of thousands of dollars and she forgets?" I can only pray that Charlie and Jack Warner were not watching and even as I think it, I know they have. Tomorrow will not be a fun day at the office.

At that moment, the doorbell rings. I am startled. Our doorbell never rings. I share a look with Bunny. She, too, is puzzled.

A neighbor? Not at this hour. I get up and go to the door. When I open it I discover Oswald and Maybelle.

"I hope this isn't a bad time," Oswald says. His visage is serious. Something is up.

"Come in," I say.

They enter. As Maybelle walks by me, she is grim faced. She is clutching a shoebox to her bosom. Oswald just shakes his head.

I introduce Bunny and offer refreshments. No one is interested. Maybelle sits at the end of the sofa, still clutching the shoebox. She has yet to speak. Bunny excuses herself. I tell her it's not necessary but she insists. She has reading to catch up on in the bedroom. When she's gone, Oswald, who has yet to sit, says to me, "Maybelle has something to show you."

She looks up at me, her expression troubled. "I was in the bungalow still sorting through everything when the manager came by. He told me that Leon and Virginia had stored some things in the basement of the main building. I thanked him and when I got a chance I went to take a look. There wasn't much there of interest except for these." She hands me the box.

"Maybe I will have a beer," Oswald says.

"Help yourself," I say, pointing toward the kitchen.

I sit down in our one and only easy chair and open the box. Inside are maybe a dozen letters tied together with a green silk ribbon.

"Love letters?" I say.

"Of a sort," Maybelle says.

They are all in their original envelopes and I see from the top one that it is addressed to Leon Schroeder c/o Wilder at Robert Wilder's New York City address. The return address is C. Schroeder at an address in Brentwood.

"Letters from mama," I say.

Maybelle merely nods. Oswald returns with his beer and sits on the other end of the sofa.

I pull out the first letter. As I read I frown in disbelief. I read second and a third. They are all alike. I look over at Oswald and Maybelle.

"These are vicious," I say.

Oswald nods. "The ravings of a possessive mother betrayed by an unloving son. Or at least that's the way she sees it."

Maybelle fixes me with a hard stare. "The things she says about Virginia. Undiluted hatred. Total evil. If you are looking for a motive for murder there it is."

I look back down at the letters. She is right. These are the ravings of a deranged woman but who could have known? On the surface, she seems kind and supportive and understanding. Beneath is a woman consumed by a pervasive sickness that saw Virginia as the spawn of Satan, a handmaiden of evil, sucking the goodness from her son, alienating him from a loving mother, browbeating him into becoming something he was not, robbing him of his manhood and self respect. On and on she went, letter after letter, never letting up.

One can only imagine what he was going through, torn between this possessive harridan and the woman he loved. How much could this have contributed to his heart attack? A great deal, I am thinking. I look over at Oswald.

"What do you think?" I ask.

"She killed Virginia," he says.

"We can't prove it," I say.

"I know. As evidence, the letters mean nothing."

"There must be something we can do," Maybelle says. She's on the verge of tears. I knew from the start how much she cared for Virginia. Maybe her affection ran deeper than any of us realized. I feel great pity for her.

"Short of a confession, we are helpless," Oswald says.

"And how could we possibly get her to confess?" I say aloud.

"No way that I know of," Oswald says.

My mind is spinning. A thought occurred to me, then flitted away, then came back. A germ of a notion. I get up and go into the kitchen where I get myself another beer even as I mull over the idea that is growing in possibility in my brain. I uncap the beer and take a long pull as I walk back into the living room. I look from Oswald to Maybelle.

"Have either of you ever heard of Patty MacLean?" I ask.

They shake their heads.

I proceed to tell them who Patty MacLean is.

CHAPTER TWENTY ONE

The first thing I do when I hit the office is to put in a call to Patty MacLean. I'm lucky. Most days she's out working. Today she's home. I make a date with her for five o'clock at the Biltmore bar. I have a job for her but she's fussy about what she'll take. Before I offer it I am going ply her with booze. Patty loves her booze but you'd never know it. In the four years I've known her I've never seen her tipsy, even after I've watched her down a half dozen pina coladas.

As soon as I hang up I'm on my way to Bert and Eleanor's kitchen.

The gal from Redbook's going to meet me there with her own photographer and I'm bringing along Buddy Raskin for backup. The Pathe newsreel crew should be already there setting up lights. Eleanor's laid in a lot of food stuffs which the studio's going to pay for. By the time I arrive everything's in place. She's wearing a gorgeous green outfit which really sets off her red hair. Every time I see her I am in awe of her vivacity and her youth. Her husband Bert is one lucky guy.

For one of the few times in my career, a complicated shoot like this goes off without a hitch. Eleanor actually cooks a cheese souffle and after all the photos are taken, we get a chance to sample it. Heaven. She also whips up a batch of oatmeal raisin cookies. Perfect. Bert clowns around wearing an apron and a toque. The Redbook reporter is ecstatic. The Pathe people chew up lots of film. By two o'clock we are done. Eleanor hugs me, so grateful for this opportunity to show off her homemaking skills. Bert shakes my hand enthusiastically and tells me he'll drop by early next week. He's got some more swell ideas we should discuss. I tell him I can't wait.

Back at my desk at the studio I reach into the bottom drawer and take out the box full of Charlotte Schroeder's letters to her son. One by one I read them. I am slow and deliberate, absorbing everything and then I reach for a yellow lined legal pad and start to take notes.

At five past five I walk into the Biltmore bar. Patty's easy to spot. She's sitting in a booth near the back. In front of her is a bulbous glass with a wedge of pineapple hung on its rim along with a paper umbrella. She sees me and waves. I wave back as I head over.

As I said, Patty's easy to spot. She's a hefty gal, not particularly tall, and round all over. I'd put her weight at maybe 175 but she's not fat so much as she's built like a nose tackle. I've heard she's a black belt in karate. I have no wish to find out first hand. Her sole weakness seems to be fruity drinks with little umbrellas. Promise her a mai tai and she'll follow you anywhere.

"Hiya, big boy, sit down and make myself comfortable," she says, doing an impeccable Mae West. I laugh because I'm supposed to but also because she is a genuinely funny lady.

"You started without me," I say. slipping into the booth.

"Funny, that's the same thing I said to the last guy I had up to my apartment," she says and I laugh again.

Patty MacLean is probably the most successful Hollywood

actress you've never had the pleasure of seeing on the big screen. If Lon Chaney was the man of a thousand faces, then Patty is the gal of a thousand voices. Everyone in the business knows her. She's been doing star voices for years, not as a night club act but behind the scenes for the studios and she's worked for all of them. The bulk of it is dubbing. Star gets laryngitis, star is on location overseas in a remote jungle, star is mad at director and won't cooperate. Worst case, star died. Patty's hired to do her voice. Two years ago a picture couldn't be released because the sound track was unusable. The star was in an auto accident and wound up in a lengthy coma. Patty dubbed her entire performance. No one knew the difference. Not the public, not the critics, not even her co-stars. Mae West? Easy. Marlene? A cinch. Marjorie Main? No problem. But Joan Crawford or Olivia DeHavilland or Celeste Holm? Nobody does these ladies. Nobody but Patty that is. What a life. No cameras, no makeup, no wardrobe and she's rolling in money.

The waitress comes by and I order a Coors.

Patty smirks. "Really, Joseph, you are too,too plebian for my company. Henceforth consider yourself persona non grata," I smile. 'Kate Hepburn' has joined us at the table.

"Dames who drink fruit juice aren't exactly part of the upper crust," I tell her.

"My doctor put me on a fruit and vegetable diet, Joe. Every night I dine on cauliflower, broccoli and cabbage." She raises her glass. "These little beverages take care of the other half."

It goes like this until my beer arrives and then I tell her it's time to get down to business. To Patty, business means money and the joshing ceases.

"What's the picture, Joe?" she asks.

"No picture, Patty. This is a very special job and there's not a lot of money involved. Only what I can spare out of my own pocket."

She hesitates, then downs the rest of her drink and signals our waitress for another. "Okay," she says, "tell me about it."

I start in. I tell her everything and when I mention murder, her eyes widen. When I tell her what I need from her, she grins. She's hooked.

We meet on Saturday morning at Maybelle's office. We debate long and hard about who should extend the invitation. In the end it falls to Oswald.

Later that afternoon we reconvene at my house and Oswald recounts in detail his meeting with Charlotte Schroeder.

"She was gracious and made me feel at home," Oswald says, "but from the beginning I could sense that she was wary. She kept asking, a tribute to Virginia? What sort of tribute? I carefully explained to her that the radio station, KFI-FM which had originally aired her poetic readings during the holiday season, had come upon a transcription of poems that somehow had gotten lost in the mix. Given the glowing eulogy offered up by the renowned poet, Jesse T. Humphreys, in the Times article, it only seemed fitting that the station honor Virginia in death as they had in life."

"Well stated and logical," I say. "Very nice, Oswald."

"Not quite nice enough, Joe. She still had reservations. It wasn't until I told her that the new poems were all paeans of praise to Leon that she relented. I think the kicker was my telling her that if she felt she wasn't up to introducing the missing poems, I was sure that Emma, Leon's widow, would be more than happy to participate. I think I heard her teeth gnash."

"So it's set then?" Maybelle asks.

"Tomorrow afternoon at two. She thinks we'll be taping for broadcast at midnight tomorrow night."

Maybelle is apprehensive. "Are you sure this is going to work?" she asks.

Oswald shakes his head. "There's no guarantee, Maybelle. We can only hope."

"Patty's been studying Virginia's voice all day from those first transcriptions. She called me an hour ago using Virginia's voice. It was scary how real it seemed."

Maybelle nods. "I hope you're right."

"What about tonight?" Oswald asks.

"Patty's going to call her three times. Seven, nine and just before midnight. She'll ask to speak to Leon. Depending on how Charlotte responds Patty will ad lib something and then hang up. The idea is to throw her off balance so she can't handle the situation at the station."

"I don't know. Charlotte's pretty sharp," Maybelle says.

"Yes, she is, Maybelle," I say, "but she's got a blind spot. Her pain at losing Leon and her vicious hatred of Virginia. She won't behave rationally."

"The other woman, Joe? No problem?" Oswald asks.

"Maddie'll be at the station an hour early. The wardrobe's a perfect fit. She knows what to do."

"I just hope Charlotte doesn't go after her," Oswald says.

"She'll never get close enough and if she does, Maddie's a stunt woman. She can handle herself." I look at the two of them. Both had loved Virginia in different ways and both had been devastated by her death. "It's not too late to call this off," I say.

Maybelle shakes her head. "No. You're right, Mr. Bernardi. It's our only shot. We have nothing else."

Oswald nods in agreement.

At ten minutes to two I am standing by the main entrance of the radio station as the DeSoto pulls into the parking lot and

Charlotte Schroeder gets out. She's wearing a conservative light green wool suit with shoes to match. On her head is a black wide brimmed straw hat. A white ribbon is wrapped around the crown and also hangs down a foot or so at the back. The ribbon is decorated with green shamrocks. Atop the crown is a tiny little 'bag of gold' closed up with a wee drawstring.

I move to meet her as she approaches.

"Mrs. Schroeder, we are all so happy to have you joining us in this tribute. Thank you for coming."

She's wearing makeup but it isn't helping. Her skin is pale and her features are drawn. Patty's phone calls seem to have unnerved her.

"Yes, yes," she says impatiently. "Let's get this over with as quickly as possible."

We go inside. The lobby of the station is small. There is a reception desk off to the right next to side by side elevators. On the left side of the lobby is a staircase leading to the second floor. Part of the upstairs corridor is open and looks down on the lobby. That is where Maddie Wicker is standing, wearing one of Virginia's distinctive dresses and leaning on the railing staring down at us. Her frame is the same as Virginia's and the wig we've given her is perfect. I look up and if I didn't know better I would swear it was Virginia returned from the grave. We are hoping Charlotte will spot Maddie on her own but if not, Oswald is up there with a tin can which he will clatter onto the ersatz marble floor. It'll be loud enough to shake windows. We've practiced.

We don't need the can. Charlotte looks up on her own and as she sees Maddie, she grabs at my arm and holds tight. Maddie meets her look momentarily and then walks off, disappearing from view.

"What's the matter?" I ask. Her grip is unrelenting. She looks up at me. There is genuine fear in her eyes. She doesn't answer. "Charlotte, what is it?"

She looks back up at the second level and then shakes her head. "Nothing," she says.

We check in with reception and then take the elevator to the second floor. When we arrive, Charlotte exits the elevator cab cautiously. The corridor is deserted. Because it's Saturday none of the business staff is on hand. Only a couple of studios are in use. We have one of them. In the other the host is playing recordings of famous operatic arias and providing commentary before and after each one.

I escort Charlotte into Studio B via a glass door in a mostly glass wall that adjoins the corridor. The room is small with a sofa and a couple of easy chairs. In the center of the room is a table. A microphone has been set up on it. Overlooking this set up is the control room with its panoply of switches and rheostats and gadgetry. Two men are busily at work. One is Jimmy DiCorso who works for Warner Brothers as a mixer. The other man is Aaron Kleinschmidt who works as a homicide detective for the Los Angeles Police Department. The regular staff of KFI-FM knows what we are up to but they are not participating.

Jimmy flips a switch so that he can be heard in the studio. He greets us affably over a loudspeaker and tells us it'll be another fifteen minutes or so until we're ready to go. I tell him no problem. I offer to fetch Charlotte some coffee or tea. She demurs.

I reach in my pocket and take out a single sheet of paper. I have taken the liberty of writing out a suggested introduction to Virginia's poems but quickly assure Charlotte that she is free to amend what I've written any way she chooses or to ignore it altogether. I have laced the text with phrases like "Virginia will never die" and "She will live on in our hearts and our memories" and "her spirit will be with us always". In handing her the intro I have positioned myself so that she can look directly past me through the glass wall and into the corridor. Charlotte is skimming the material but as she looks up, I see her stiffen and I hear a muffled gasp and I know that Maddie is walking slowly by, staring straight ahead. At the last moment that she is within Charlotte's line of sight she will turn her head and for the merest of instants, look directly into Charlotte's eyes.

"No," Charlotte croaks quietly.

I lean in as if I haven't heard.

"Did you say something?"

She is frozen, staring past me. Then she looks up. "Water," she says. "I could use glass of water."

"Coming up," I say. "There's a water cooler in the control room."

I cross to the control room door and exit leaving Charlotte alone in the studio. As soon as the door shuts, Jimmy pushes a button which will start to feed Patty MacLean's voice into the studio. The volume will be low and the quality mildly distorted with a hint of echo and just a tiny bit of static. Having worked with Patty on this recording, I know exactly what Charlotte is listening to.

".... dear beloved Leon, you mean so much to me but you must tear yourself away from her. She is smothering you. How can you live, dear one, even as she crushes your spirit and sucks the life from your being. This is not the love of a mother, this is the selfish possessiveness of a bitter and lonely old woman...."

I am watching Charlotte carefully. She is sitting erect now, disbelieving what she is hearing. It is more than just Virginia's voice returned from the dead, it is the words she is speaking.

I have taken Charlotte's damning condemnation of Virginia and twisted it around so that now Virginia is saying these things to Leon that Charlotte had written in the letters to her son. Charlotte tries to rise from her chair. She grips the table unsteadily.

I open the control room door and return carrying a glass of water. When the door opened, Virginia had gone silent. I put the glass on the table and feign concern.

"Are you all right?" I ask.

She looks at me, eyes displaying the madness within.

"She's dead," Charlotte says quietly. "She's dead."

I look puzzled. "Who? Virginia?"

"Yes. That woman. Virginia. She's dead."

"Of course she's dead," I say. "Charlotte, what is it? What's wrong?"

"Nothing."

"You're pale and you're sweating. Drink some water."

"I don't want any water!" she says hysterically.

Virginia's low level voice begins again.

"....as long as you stay under her thumb, as long as allow her to rule your life, you will never realize your potential. You must escape her now.

"You must act, my darling. The evil one must be destroyed...."

I put my hand out to her. She shrugs me off furiously. "You hear it. You must hear it!" she says loudly.

"Hear what?"

"Her voice! You must hear her voice!"

"I don't hear anything. Charlotte, for Gods sakes, get a hold of yourself."

I try again to calm her. She backs away. At that moment Maddie again walks by the window looking straight ahead, paying Charlotte no mind. Charlotte charges the window and starts to pound on it. "Leave me alone!" she wails. I go to her trying to pull her away from the window. Virginia's voice continues, barely audible.

"....she must be destroyed. If you haven't the courage, I do. Act now, my loved one, before it is too late, before her tentacles have strangled us both. She cannot be allowed to live....."

Charlotte is backing across the room, shaking her head violently. I pick up the water glass and go after her sternly.

"Stop it! You're behaving like a mad woman!" I shout.

I extend the water to her. Then I extend my other hand. A closed fist. I open it under her nose to reveal a capsule identical to Virginia's medicine and identical to the one that killed her.

Charlotte stares at it in horror and gasps. She slaps my hand away, then falls to her knees. She begins to wail as tears pour forth from her eyes. "I destroyed her," she gasps quietly. "I destroyed her. She is dead. I destroyed her. She is dead. I destroyed her." Softly, over and over she repeats this mantra.

Kleinschmidt and Jimmy emerge from the control room and help me get her onto the sofa. Her face is eggshell white and she is having trouble breathing as she keeps repeating it, over and over. "...I destroyed her, she is dead..."

Jimmy walks over to the table and turns off the microphone. It's been 'hot' ever since we walked into the room and everything that has been said has been recorded on magnetic tape.

Kleinschmidt has been kneeling beside Charlotte whose eyes seem blank and unfocused. He frowns and looks at me. "Call an ambulance. Tell 'em to make it quick."

CHAPTER TWENTY TWO

Charlotte Schroeder didn't die that day. Or the next. Or the day after that. After being taken to Metro Division and booked, she was given a cursory examination by a police psychiatrist. On his recommendation she was transfered to County General's psychiatric ward for observation.

It is three days later. Oswald and I have met for lunch at Musso & Franks (nobody calls it The Musso & Frank Grill) on Hollywood Boulevard. When I have to entertain off the lot for lunch, this is my most frequent destination. Its walls reek of the celebrities that have eaten here, particularly my personal icons like Fitzgerald, Hemingway, Faulkner and Raymond Chandler. And I always make sure I get a booth where Theo Parfrey will be my waiter. Theo is old enough to be my grandfather and I've been told, though he won't admit it, that he was one of the original waiters back in 1919 when the place opened. Scrawny, balding and slow afoot, he makes Oswald seem almost young. While we are waiting for our third luncheon companion, Theo relates an amusing story about Orson Welles who used to hold court here on a regular basis, trying to raise money for his various projects. Oswald counters by recalling the day Bat Masterson showed up in Ukiah and interviewed him for the New York

Morning Telegraph. Theo responds that Scott Fitzgerald once asked him for background color for a short story he was writing about an unsuccessful restaurant. Oswald happened to remember a snowy night in December in the woods when he was able to fight off a grizzly bear with nothing but a pen knife. Theo was about to top that one when I sent him scurrying off to bring back a couple of cold brews.

Oswald is forced to laugh and allows that he kind of likes the old geezer. Just then our third shows up and Aaron Kleinschmidt slips into the booth next to Oswald. He apologizes for being late. They just pulled a naked body out of a swimming pool at a mansion off Franklin Avenue a few doors down from The Magic Castle. Murder most foul. He asks me if I have an alibi for the hours between four and six in the morning. Then he laughs. I laugh with him. I have a certain reputation with the LAPD and it makes me a little nervous.

Theo returns with our beer. Kleinschmidt orders a black coffee. We ask Theo to give us a a few minutes. Oswald and I are here to get a report that only Kleinschmidt can give us.

"This is all confidential," he says. "Either of you guys breathe a word and it could be my badge." Oswald and I raise our right hands, three fingers displayed, and promise to be trustworthy, loyal and brave and also to keep our mouths shut.

"The doctor's name is Breslin. He says she's mentally unstable but he's not sure her condition rises to the level of clinically insane. However, there is no doubt that she killed Virginia. In fact she is now admitting it, somewhat proudly, Breslin says. She tampered with the capsule and placed it in the bottle a couple of weeks after her son had died. She was filled with hate but a cold calculating hate. She was going to have her revenge on the woman whose constant prodding and pressuring led to Leon's fatal heart attack. She had wheedled her way into Virginia's confidence to get access to the medicine cabinet and afterwards kept up appearances to deflect suspicion in case poison was found."

"Well, she had me fooled," I say.

"Along with everyone else," Kleinschmidt says.

"So what's going to happen?" Oswald asks.

"A panel of doctors will examine her to determine her sanity and also if she is fit to stand trial. She'll probably remain at County General for a while and if they find that she cannot be tried, she'll be admitted to the facility at Camarillo."

"Sad," Oswald says.

"Sadder stlll for Virginia," I say.

That's one thing we could all agree on.

I'm back in my office by three o'clock. I hear Janie Wyman's back in town but she hasn't called. Eleanor's husband Bert is coming by tomorrow morning. God only knows what he has in store for me. As for Gertrude Lawrence, not a peep.

The phone rings. Glenda Mae tells me it's Maybelle Ruskin. Put her through, I say.

"Mr. Bernardi, I just called to thank you."

"Not necessary." I say.

"Oh, but it is," she says. "I thank you not only for myself but for Virginia whose legacy will now live on after the ugliness of the past few days has been long forgotten."

"I'm not sure I follow you, Maybelle," I say.

"Her books, Mr. Bernardi. Her poems. They are selling out. We are receiving reports from book stores all over the Southland. They cannot keep them on the shelves. They are clamoring for more."

"That's wonderful," I say with enthusiasm, wondering why.

"In death she is becoming an icon like Phillis Wheatly or Ella Wheeler Wilcox."

"Who?" I ask, totally at sea.

Ignoring me, she continues. "The publisher is rushing to put out new editions of all her existing works and plans a major campaign to promote her new volume of heretofore unpublished works."

"Those would be the poems you rescued from her trash bin," I suggest.

Her voice takes on a huffy edge. "Call them what you like, Mr. Bernardi, her publisher loves them all."

"I'm sure he does," I say.

"In any event, I am writing a brief forward for the new volume thanking you and Mr. Pennybaker for bringing her killer to justice. I'm sure you have no objection."

"None whatsoever," I say.

"And, of course, I will be sending you a copy of the first edition," she tells me.

"Thrilled," I say. I almost said, "Autographed?" but caught myself in time. Call me prudish but I think there is something a little unseemly about cashing in on the notoriety engendered by this cruel murder. It feels a little like civilized graverobbing. There are times when the almighty dollar should take a back seat to the better side of our nature. I wonder, would it be kinder to let Virginia rest in peace or would she opt for this postmortem adulation if she had anything to say about it? Maybe I'd feel easier about it if her poems were better. Or maybe they are better and I don't know it. A distinct possibility.

Minding my manners I thank Maybelle for her call and wish her luck.

I sit quietly for a few minutes thinking over what I have been through over the past few days. I realize I am tired I need quiet and I need sleep and I seriously consider taking tomorrow off.

This coming Monday we start principal photography on 'The Glass Menagerie'. Everything is well in hand. There is nothing that needs to be done that can't wait. Maybe I can talk Bunny into a couple of days of hookie at some little hideaway inn up in Santa Cruz where we can eat, sleep and make love without benefit of a noisy telephone. Not strangely, this is one of Bunny's favorite things to do. She'll leap at it and the more I think about it, the better I like it.

I get up from my desk and head out. On the way I tell Glenda Mae to take the rest of the day off and that I may take tomorrow off and maybe even the day after and if anybody asks she doesn't know where I am which will be the truth because I'm not going to tell her. She gives me a patronizing smile. She's seen me like this before. Little does she know that this time I mean it. She picks up an envelope from her desk and tells me it just arrived from Henry Blanke. I might want to read it before I disappear for the foreseeable future,

I take it from her and open it hopefully. I start to read. Henry has read my novel. He likes it. He thinks it will make an excellent movie. I smile. This is what I wanted to hear. He suggests I get my agent to get it to a book publisher immediately. Once a book deal is made, Warner's will option it for filming. This should be no problem. The Virginia Jenks murder case is a major story. The public is enthralled.Their thirst for details has been insatiable. We must act right away to take advantage of this publicity. By playing up the plagiarism angle and the subsequent poisoning and my involvement in the solving of Virginia's death, the promotional hook is a natural. It can't miss.

I stare at Henry's memo for the longest time and then slowly I wad it up and toss it in Glenda Mae's wastepaper basket.

"First thing tomorrow," I tell her, "send a memo over my

name to Mr. Blanke expressing my gratitude for his enthusiastic reaction to my book and his suggestions for marketing it. While I am away from the office I will give all of his ideas a great deal of thought." I won't, of course. If 'A Family of Strangers' can't thrive on its own, then to hell with it.

I head for home. Bunny's beaten me there by fifteen minutes. I lay out my swell plan for dropping out. She's all for it. Billy owes her some time off. No problem. She digs in the bottom drawer of the desk and pulls out several dozen brochures promoting getaway retreats with low cost package deals. We start sifting through them. And then the phone rings. Bunny answers it, then hands it to me. It's Gertrude's husband, Richard Aldrich.

"Joe," he says heartily.

"Richard," I respond, just as heartily.

"Did I catch you at a bad time?"

"Absolutely not," I say. "Where are you?"

I listen intently.

"Really?" I say. "The weather must be a little chilly there although I doubt it's very crowded this time of year."

I listen some more.

"Richard, I would love to discuss this with you at some length but Bunny and I were just heading out the door. Our neighborhood theater is having a revival showing of an old Fox picture, "Anna and the King of Siam" and we don't want to miss the beginning."

I listen, feigning both surprise and enthusiasm.

"Is that right? I had no idea. What a coincidence."

More listening.

"Whats My Line? No, I'm afraid we missed it. There was a power outage in the neighborhood for almost two hours. I'm very disappointed. I was looking forward to seeing it."

And yet more listening.

"Well, yes, the celebration to the Snow Gods by the indigenous natives sounds fascinating but I doubt we could arrange anything by noon tomorrow. Tell you what, call me at the office in the morning and we'll see what we can work out and meanwhile, best of everything to Gertrude. I can't tell you how much she's been in my thoughts these past few days."

I hang up and turn to Bunny with a smile. She smiles back and then holds up a brochure.

"Huge double bed, view of the ocean, breakfast included, free television in the room and----" She wiggles her eyebrows provocatively.

"And?" I say.

"A mirror on the ceiling over the bed."

I look to see if she's kidding. She's not. I hand her the phone. "Book it."

THE END

AUTHOR'S NOTE

The Oscar is the trademarked award handed out each year by the Academy of Motion Picture Arts and Sciences. It is the most honored and sought after award of all those bestowed within the motion picture community. Little wonder that everyone wants one. As ever, this is a work of fiction and all scenes involving well known personalities of the era have been totally invented by the author who has nothing but the highest regard for them all. In the Oscar competition for 1950 neither Gertrude Lawrence nor Jane Wyman received a nomination although Eleanor Parker was cited for her work in "Caged". Both Anne Baxter and Bette Davis were nominated for "All About Eve" as was Gloria Swanson for her performance in "Sunset Boulevard". However it was Judy Holliday who walked off with the prize for "Born Yesterday". Sometimes comediennes DO win. Eleanor Parker went on to receive two more Oscar nods as did Jane Wyman. Gertrude Lawrence was never nominated although the following year she won Broadway's Tony Award for "The King and I". Arthur Kennedy was nominated a total of five times, never winning. Kirk Douglas was tapped three times. He, too, never won although in 1996 the Academy honored him with a special award for a lifetime of work. As for Jack Warner, "The Glass Menagerie" was not nominated and he would have to wait another fourteen years before the studio was finally awarded another Best Picture Oscar for "My Fair Lady."

MISSING SOMETHING?

The first three books in the Hollywood Murder Mystery series are still available from Grove Point Press at a low introductory price of $9.95 each. All copies will be personally signed and dated by the author. If you purchase ALL THREE at $29.85 for the set, you will automatically become a member of "the club". This means that you will be able to buy all subsequent volumes at the $9.95 price, a savings of $3.00 over the regular cover price of $12.95. This offer is confined to direct purchases from The Grove Point Press and does not apply to other on-line sites which may carry the series.

Book One—1947
JEZEBEL IN BLUE SATIN

WWII is over and Joe Bernardi has just returned home after three years as a war correspondent in Europe. Married in the heat of passion three weeks before he shipped out, he has come home to find his wife Lydia a complete stranger. It's not long before Lydia is off to Reno for a quickie divorce which Joe won't accept. Meanwhile he's been hired as a publicist by third rate movie studio, Continental Pictures. One night he enters a darkened sound stage only to discover the dead body of ambitious, would-be actress Maggie Baumann. When the police investigate, they immediately zero in on Joe as the perp. Short on evidence they attempt to frame him and almost succeed. Who really killed Maggie? Was it the over-the-hill actress trying for a comeback? Or the talentless director with delusions of grandeur? Or maybe it was the hapless leading man whose career is headed nowhere now that the "real stars" are coming back from the war. There is no shortage of suspects as the story speeds along to its exciting and unexpected conclusion.

Book Two—1948
WE DON'T NEED NO STINKING BADGES

Joe Bernardi is the new guy in Warner Brothers' Press Department so it's no surprise when Joe is given the unenviable task of flying to Tampico, Mexico, to bail Humphrey Bogart out of jail without the world learning about it. When he arrives he discovers that Bogie isn't the problem. So-called accidents are occurring daily on the set, slowing down the filming of "The Treasure of the Sierra Madre" and putting tempers on edge. Everyone knows who's behind the sabotage. It's the local Jefe who has a finger in every illegal pie. But suddenly the intrigue widens and the murder of one of the actors throws the company into turmoil. Day by day, Joe finds himself drawn into a dangerous web of deceit, dupliciity and blackmail that nearly costs him his life.

Book Three—1949
LOVE HAS NOTHING TO DO WITH IT

Joe Bernardi's ex-wife Lydia is in big, big trouble. On a Sunday evening around midnight she is seen running from the plush offices of her one-time lover, Tyler Banks. She disappears into the night leaving Banks behind, dead on the carpet with a bullet in his head. Convinced that she is innocent, Joe enlists the help of his pal, lawyer Ray Giordano, and bail bondsman Mick Clausen, to prove Lydia's innocence, even as his assignment to publicize Jimmy Cagney's comeback movie for Warner's threatens to take up all of his time. Who really pulled the trigger that night? Was it the millionaire whose influence reached into City Hall? Or the not so grieving widow finally freed from a loveless marriage. Maybe it was the partner who wanted the business all to himself as well as the new widow. And what about the mysterious envelope, the one that disappeared and everyone claims never existed? Is it the key to the killer's identity and what is the secret that has been kept hidden for the past forty years?

Order any one of the above for the low introductory price of $9.95. Order all three for $29.85 and "join the club" giving you the privilege of purchasing all subsequent books in the series for $9.95 as opposed to the cover price of $12.95. This offer applies only to purchases made directly by check or money order to The Grove Point Press, P.O.Box 873, Pacific Grove, CA 93950. All books personally signed by the author. The price per book includes all taxes as well as shipping and handling.

COMING SOON!
Book Five—1951
THE UNKINDNESS OF STRANGERS

ABOUT THE AUTHOR

Peter S. Fischer is a former television writer-producer who currently lives with his wife Lucille in the Monterey Bay area of Central California. He is a co-creator of "Murder, She Wrote" for which he wrote over 40 scripts. Among his other credits are a dozen "Columbo" episodes and a season helming "Ellery Queen". He has also written and produced several TV miniseries and Movies of the Week. In 1985 he was awarded an Edgar by the Mystery Writers of America. "Everybody Wants an Oscar" is the fourth in a series of murder mysteries set in post WWII Hollywood and featuring publicist and would-be novelist, Joe Bernardi.

TO ORDER ADDITIONAL COPIES

If your local bookseller is out of stock, you may order additional copies of this book through The Grove Point Press, P.O. Box 873, Pacific Grove, California 93950. Enclose check or money order for $12.95. We pay shipping, handling and any taxes required. Order 3 or more copies and take a 10% discount. 8 or more, take 20%. You may also obtain copies via the internet through Amazon and other sites which offer a paperback edition as well as electronic versions. All copies purchased directly from The Grove Point Press will be personally signed and dated by the author.